ANOTHER LONG RUN

A Novel for Young Adults

Best Wishes,
Ed Koch

Edward R. Koch

WESTBOW
PRESS®
A DIVISION OF THOMAS NELSON
& ZONDERVAN

Copyright © 2024 Edward R. Koch.

All rights reserved. No part of this book may be used or reproduced by any means, graphic, electronic, or mechanical, including photocopying, recording, taping or by any information storage retrieval system without the written permission of the author except in the case of brief quotations embodied in critical articles and reviews.

This is a work of fiction. All of the characters, names, incidents, organizations, and dialogue in this novel are either the products of the author's imagination or are used fictitiously.

WestBow Press books may be ordered through booksellers or by contacting:

WestBow Press
A Division of Thomas Nelson & Zondervan
1663 Liberty Drive
Bloomington, IN 47403
www.westbowpress.com
844-714-3454

Because of the dynamic nature of the Internet, any web addresses or links contained in this book may have changed since publication and may no longer be valid. The views expressed in this work are solely those of the author and do not necessarily reflect the views of the publisher, and the publisher hereby disclaims any responsibility for them.

Any people depicted in stock imagery provided by Getty Images are models, and such images are being used for illustrative purposes only.
Certain stock imagery © Getty Images.

Scripture is taken from the NEW AMERICAN STANDARD BIBLE®, Copyright © 1960, 1962, 1963, 1968, 1971, 1972, 1973, 1975, 1977, 1995 by The Lockman Foundation. Used by permission.

ISBN: 979-8-3850-3159-7 (sc)
ISBN: 979-8-3850-3160-3 (hc)
ISBN: 979-8-3850-3161-0 (e)

Library of Congress Control Number: 2024916903

Print information available on the last page.

WestBow Press rev. date: 11/14/2024

DEDICATION

To the 1976 SJR Track & Field Team

They also persevered.

And

To Bob Murphy, My High School Coach

And

Jim Tuppeny, My College Coach

They taught me the sport.

CONTENTS

Chapter 1   August 1
Chapter 2   August (Continued) 4
Chapter 3   Labor Day 7
Chapter 4   Early September 10
Chapter 5   Mid September 17
Chapter 6   Late September 23
Chapter 7   Early October 28
Chapter 8   Early October (Continued) 33
Chapter 9   Mid October 35
Chapter 10   Mid October (Continued) 40
Chapter 11   Late October 46
Chapter 12   Early November 49
Chapter 13   Early November (Continued) 52
Chapter 14   Early November (Still Continued) 55
Chapter 15   Mid November 59
Chapter 16   Late November 61
Chapter 17   Early December 63
Chapter 18   Early December (Continued) 69
Chapter 19   Mid December 73
Chapter 20   Holidays 80
Chapter 21   Holidays (Continued) 83
Chapter 22   Early January 88
Chapter 23   Mid January 91
Chapter 24   Late January 94

Chapter 25 Early February 97

Chapter 26 Mid February 103

Chapter 27 Late February 106

Chapter 28 Early March..112

Chapter 29 Early March (Continued)...116

Chapter 30 Mid March 118

Chapter 31 Late March 121

Chapter 32 Early April 124

Chapter 33 Mid April 129

Chapter 34 Late April 132

Chapter 35 Late April (Continued) 140

Chapter 36 Early May 146

Chapter 37 Mid May 150

Chapter 38 Mid May (Continued) 157

Chapter 39 Late May 161

Chapter 40 June 167

Afterward 173

CHAPTER ONE: AUGUST

"The whole thing stinks!"

The cross country and track & field captains felt the round table shake in the Stewarts' basement as Chuck James pounded it with his fist.

"We are in agreement that the situation smells awful," replied Artie Stewart with a smile. "The question is what do we do about it?"

"I don't know," said Sean Allen. "I did not sign up for this when I said I would be the co-captain of the cross country team with you, Artie. I should have just stuck with my race walking this season."

"Yeah, and it will be even worse when we get to the track & field season," added Bruce Griffin.

"Lighten up," sighed Artie. "Why don't we write a list of all the problems we've got and how we can try to fix them."

"Alright," answered Sean. "Start with the fact that our Athletic Director Buddy McGurk has given us a substitute coach that knows nothing about running except that Mr. Wimble and his wife like to jog in the morning. What are we going to do about workouts?"

"We can deal with that," replied Artie. We know a lot about distance training already. You and I kept training logs during cross country the last two years. We can politely suggest workouts to Mr. Wimble to approve."

"And when we get to the track & field season, I can ask my brother Ted for the workouts that Coach Mallory used to give the sprinters and 400/800 guys. And he can ask his former teammates about workouts in the hurdles and field events." (As the only one at the table who was a captain for both cross country and track & field, Artie was already thinking about the full year, not just one season – and he knew he could rely on his older brother for help.)

"Well, that might work," said Bruce. "But what about the size of the squad? We need more guys than we currently have for cross country. We have both of you plus Tommy O'Leary for our top three, but not much after that. We need solid fourth and fifth runners for the scoring plus two more for the varsity seven not to mention the junior varsity or frosh. And do not look at me. I am a hurdler, not a distance runner."

"I thought you might want to prep for the college steeplechase," quipped Artie. "We do need to get more sophs from last year's frosh team to try out. They have been spotty coming to summer practices even if those practices are voluntary."

"We do need to attract a bunch of frosh. Not to help the varsity this year, but to make sure the team has potential after we graduate. In short, we need to do some more recruiting of our fellow schoolmates."

"Even if we get some good workouts set up and fill out a decent sized squad, the schedule that our AD McGurk has set up is terrible," complained Sean. "It has just dual & tri meets before the league, county, and district meets. How are we going to be ready without doing some weekend invitational meets early in the season? The younger guys especially need to learn about running in packs in bigger races to get ready."

"For sure, we need to talk to McGurk," mused Artie. Yes, he's a cheapskate except for his football team. But we need to run in a couple invitationals. We need an appointment to talk to him."

"Don't include me in that talk," warned Chuck James. "I am not involved in cross country anyway, and he hasn't forgiven me for quitting his football team."

"I do know one thing," added Chuck. "I like the idea of getting some info out to the team alumni. Not only do they have expertise about workouts, but they will give us moral support and maybe put a little pressure on the school. But how do we do that with Coach Mallory out of the picture right now?"

"My brother Ted says that Mrs. Mallory has always communicated information to the team alumni on behalf of Coach Mallory via email and social media. "I think if we ask her, she will get out any information about the team that we give her."

"This sounds like an awful lot to do," commented Sean woefully. "And we have not even talked about getting up our training milage. We need more miles or kilometers to be ready for the meets which are not that far away."

"It is simple when you think about it, Artie chimed-in with a smile while making some notes. "It is a five-step plan:

T is for TRAINING plans that we can create from our logs and with help from alumni.

R is RECRUITING new team members from the school to increase our squad size.

A is for an APPOINTMENT with our Athletic Director Buddy McGurk.

C is for COMMUNICATION to our team alumni with Mrs. Mallory's help; and

K is for the KILOMETERS or miles that we need to be ready for the upcoming meets."

In short, it is T-R-A-C-K and that spells TRACK! Get it?"

There were groans around the table.

"Please remember that I am a F-I-E-L-D guy. As In field events!" noted Chuck laughing.

Just then, Artie Stewart's dad came down to the basement.

"Gentlemen," he said. "Mrs. Stewart and I are having a late summer barbeque. Dinner starts in about ten minutes. You are all invited to stay even if you are finishing up your discussions down here."

The conversations about the upcoming season ended immediately as Sean, Bruce, and Chuck pulled out their phones to check with their parents. The Stewarts were known to have excellent barbeques.

CHAPTER TWO: AUGUST (CONTINUED)

Artie Stewart opened the door and headed out for another long run.

"Don't forget your water bottle," his mother called.

"I've got it," he answered.

Did his mom really think he would forget a water bottle on a warm evening like this?

That was what it was all about this time of year. Miles and miles - or kilometers and kilometers if you were metrically inclined. The "K" in the "TRACK" plan. A long run, another long run, and another long run. Another and another. Put the training in the bank now and it could pay off at the end of the season – assuming he could stay healthy.

Some of Artie's runs in August were part of the voluntary summer team practices (called "Captains' Practices") that Artie and Sean were leading until the school year started, some runs included only the trio of Artie, Sean, and Tommy O'Leary, and some were solo. Because of the daytime heat, Artie was trying to run in the early morning or late evening when it was cooler. Sometimes, he was even running both times in a single day - double workouts – to increase his mileage. This evening, Artie, Sean, and Tommy were to meet at the entrance of County Park.

Artie and Sean had immediately told Tommy about the "TRACK" plan that the captains had developed. Tommy was Green

Ridge's star half-miler but not the distance runner that the two captains were. His strategy in longer races was to try to hang with true distance runners until near the end of a race when his outstanding kick could beat many – if not most – of them.

It was good for the three of them to gather at County Park to run a few miles or kilometers. The early pace would be relaxed, and they could discuss how the "TRACK" plan was coming along after a week.

"Well," said Artie, "As far as the "T" for TRAINING is concerned, our training runs are going well, and the Captains' practices have been good with the guys who are showing up. But it is hard to say for the rest of the team. We should remind them to keep training logs and we should keep making suggestions."

"And that leads into the "R" for RECRUITMENT," Sean responded. "We certainly have all the juniors and seniors we are going to get this fall but should intensify our messages sent to the sophomores who ran on the frosh team last year. If they have been on the fence about running on the team this fall, we need to encourage them and persuade them that it is not too late to get going. But we want them to start doing mileage now. Best not to start from scratch when official practices start."

"When are you going to approach McGurk?" asked Tommy thinking about the "A" for APPOINTMENT in TRACK.

"Not before the beginning of school," answered Artie, "Right now, he is spending most of his time at football practices and he would not appreciate having us interrupt his focus at the football field."

"I have been taking care of the "C' for COMMUNICATION," said Sean, "I have started sending season preview information to Mrs. Mallory and she is already posting it on the team's social media page for the Alumni who have been responding nicely. A couple of them even have younger brothers who will be coming out for the first-year team! We need good athletes on the frosh team for the future even if they are not going to help the varsity this year."

"And that brings us to "K" for Kilometers," said Artie, "And I suggest we do something about that right now by attacking the next few miles in County Park."

With that, the trio picked up the pace and really started working the hills in the park.

CHAPTER THREE: LABOR DAY

Artie was running by himself on the evening of Labor Day. Sean and Tommy were away at the Allen Family's summer place for the holiday weekend. Artie could not join them because he had promised to work through Labor Day at his summer job. He had finished that in the afternoon and was now free to hit the roads for another long run.

Artie thought it was just as well that he was solo anyway. He needed some time to think. He had been trying to be positive talking to the guys about the upcoming year, but things had been in a downward spiral ever since Coach Mallory had gotten cancer.

Coach Mallory had been at Green Ridge High School for decades. Most years he led championship or contending teams including the years that Artie's brother Ted ran for the team. Mallory was still coaching at the end of Artie's sophomore year when he had received the cancer diagnosis.

Artie did not know exactly what kind of cancer Coach Mallory had. He knew that his mom had breast cancer when he was young, but they caught it early and she had been fine ever since. He also knew that his Uncle Fred had Multiple Myeloma (cancer in the bone marrow) a few years ago but with the help of treatments, he was in remission and seemed okay these days. On the other hand, Coach Mallory was in a fight for his life.

Unfortunately, Coach Mallory's absence had given Buddy McGurk an opening. McGurk had become the football coach a few years ago when Tony Karlan had retired. Karlan always seemed a tough but fair person whose teams had much success on the field. On the other hand, McGurk was bombastic and promised bigger and better teams every year. It was football first and everything else was an afterthought.

When Athletic Director Joe Howser retired, Green Ridge asked Bill Mallory to become the interim director. Mallory had no desire to hold the job long-term, but he filled the gap to allow time for the school to do a lengthy search. However, when Mallory had to take his leave of absence, McGurk made his move. Football parents lobbied the principal and the Board of Education. McGurk became the Athletic Director while remaining the football coach.

One of McGurk's first tasks was to find a temporary cross country and track & field coach for Artie's junior year. Angela Wright had already accepted the role of coach for the girls' team, and McGurk gave her an offer she could not refuse: to be the first woman in the school's history to coach a boys' team as well. However, after that, McGurk never found her the experienced assistant that he promised and always found an excuse to limit her budgets.

After a disappointing year, Angela Wright saw the handwriting on the wall and snapped up an offer to become an assistant coach at State University.

Now came word that Mr. and Mrs. Wimble would be the interim coaches for the boys' and girls' teams, respectively. McGurk's excuse was that the teachers' union agreement had a clause that faculty members received priority in filling coaching vacancies. Mr. Wimble told the captains that he took the position because McGurk said they might have to suspend the program if he and Mrs. Wimble did not accept.

Artie turned the corner and headed to County Park. He would be running races there as the season progressed. Presently, he saw another runner up ahead. He did not recognize the runner who looked younger than he was. He sped up to narrow the gap between them. In a couple minutes, he caught up and pulled alongside the other runner.

"Hi, my name is Artie Stewart. I do not think we have met. Are you new around here?"

"Yes, I am. My name is Ed Glavine. My family just moved here from Florida over the weekend. We are over on Maple Street.

"Did you run in Florida?"

"Yes, I did. I broke five minutes in the 1600 meters in ninth grade last year. I was hoping to run this year. My folks even sent the report of my physical up here to get clearance to try out at Green Ridge. But I am concerned about two things."

"Well, I am the co-captain of the Cross- Country team. I can be of assistance …"

"I looked online, and it shows you have a powerhouse team. I was wondering if I am good enough to join. And when I checked the school directory for your coach, it said TBA. What is up with that?"

"We are in a rebuilding transition. You would be welcome. If you bring your running gear to school tomorrow, I can introduce you to the team. Our regular coach is out sick, and Mr. Wimble is the temporary coach. I can introduce you to him too. I can also email you the form that your parents need to sign. Anything else of concern?"

"Yeah, it is real flat in Florida, and I have never seen hills like you have around here. How do you manage them."

"Like anything else, it takes practice."

Artie and Ed Glavine talked some more as they headed back to their homes. Artie told Ed about teammates, the competition in the league and county, the upcoming schedule, and more. When they got to Maple Street, Ed finished up and Artie continued to the Stewart's house a few blocks away. It had been a productive workout in more ways than one. When he got back home, he sent a message to Sean and Tommy that he had just recruited a new member of the cross-country team!

CHAPTER FOUR: EARLY SEPTEMBER

Artie woke up on the Tuesday morning after Labor Day and quickly dressed in running gear. He got outside and began to run four miles that would end at Green Ridge High School. Early in the season, he was trying to do double workouts on some days to increase his mileage. He wore a light backpack. He tried to keep as much of his schoolbooks and schoolwork on a tablet to reduce weight. Once at school, he headed to the locker room where he had a change of clothing stored in his locker.

The school day went okay. He was adjusting to the new courses: English, American History, Spanish, Advanced Math, Physics, and Phys Ed. When classes finally ended, he hustled to the locker room.

Today was the day that they would learn the size of the Green Ridge boys' cross-country squad. Sean Allen and he would find out if their summer recruiting efforts of Green Ridge students had paid off — the "R" in their "TRACK" plan. Across the way in the girls' locker room, the girls' co-captains would find out the size of the girls' team.

Two weeks earlier, twelve boys had shown up for the pre-season check-in. There were four seniors, four juniors, and four sophs. They handed in their forms, each signed by a parent or guardian, and received a check-up from a school doctor. Anyone who was away or unavailable two weeks ago needed to hand in the forms and get a check-up today.

The squad needed fourteen runners who were seniors, juniors, and sophs to have a full varsity seven and full junior varsity seven at cross country meets. However, Sean and Artie were hoping to start with more than fourteen runners to allow for the inevitable injuries, illnesses, and attrition that occur during the season.

The co-captains had especially reached out to all the sophs who had been the top seven frosh runners last year. They talked up the team to several of them when they saw them in town during the summer. Four of the seven came to the pre-season check-in. They were hoping for more today.

In the locker room, after he changed into his running gear, Artie looked at the check-in sheet. It had four more sophs in addition to the previous names: two more from last year's top seven frosh, plus Ed Glavine, and one other. That gave them sixteen on the squad excluding the frosh. A couple more would have been nice, but sixteen would do.

Artie next turned his attention to the frosh. They also needed seven runners on the roster to have a full frosh team at the meets, but they wanted more to start the season. They had sent invitations to all the incoming first-year students that had been on middle school and Junior Olympic teams or run in the Green Ridge 5K road race.

The frosh students did not have a pre-season check-in. It was anyone's guess how many of them would show up today with their signed forms. They would also get medical check-ups from the school doctor after the four sophomores. Artie counted the names on the frosh check-in sheet and was pleased that it reached double digits with a total of ten.

Presently, Mr. Wimble went outside with the twelve pre-season check-ins to the front of the school and gave a brief pep-talk. There had been voluntary team practices during summer, but official practices could only start in September according to state rules. Mr. Wimble decided to start officially today.

After Mr. Wimble finished talking, the co-captains spoke briefly and all the boys except Artie headed out on the roads to do the "Lasso" loop. Artie returned to the locker room with Mr. Wimble to await the remaining four sophomores to complete their medical check-ups.

Once the four sophomores were ready, Mr. Wimble gave them a few words of encouragement and Artie led them outside trailing the others already on the roads. Mr. Wimble stayed with the first-year boys.

After their check-ups, they would do a brief workout on the school grounds.

The first-year students would stay on the school grounds the entire week. On Friday, they would have a one-mile time trial on the track to see how advanced they were. Since Mr. Wimble had no experience with a stopwatch, the co-captains had arranged for a couple of Green Ridge alumni who were certified officials to come on Friday and do the starting and timing.

Next week, the frosh would go on the roads escorted by a couple of junior varsity runners picked on a rotating basis. One junior varsity runner would lead, and the other would trail the frosh.

Artie and the four sophs, including Ed Glavine, headed out on the roads to do a 7-mile Lasso loop. Sean and he had planned this initial workout as part of the "T" or Training plans in "TRACK."

Today's workout included the 2.5 mile "rope" portion to the County Park, then the "Lasso" portion, which was a two-mile oval around the park, and then 2.5 miles back the same way they came. Having the lasso portion on dirt and grass in the middle gave the runners' legs a respite from the hard asphalt and concrete surfaces at the beginning and end of the workout. However, some of the junior varsity runners who could not yet manage the full seven miles, would turn around at the entrance of the park and return to school doing only 5 miles.

The 7-mile loop had ups and downs with rolling hills but no heartbreak hills. Artie led the four sophs but, on the hills, pulled alongside Ed and gave him instructions. Even though the most efficient way of handling hills was for a runner to keep an even effort through the race, it did not always fit into racing strategy.

Artie explained to Ed that he should keep his body perpendicular to the plane of gravity. Going up a hill meant leaning into the hill a bit. Going down a hill meant leaning back a bit – at least with the legs. Some runners felt comfortable crouching a bit but keeping balance was imperative.

Ed seemed to catch on gradually. Before the five boys reached the park, they saw junior varsity teammates and then varsity teammates passing them on the way back.

It was good for Ed to see the full loop around the park. It covered parts of the high school course on which races would take place. Artie kept the pace level for this first workout.

Returning from the park, Artie picked up the pace, lifting on the last mile. He and Ed pulled away from the three others. It was a good start to the season.

The Wednesday workout went well too. The squad did one-mile repeats on the school grounds. The varsity (including wannabes) did five, the junior varsity did four, and the first-year students did three.

On Thursday, Sean and Artie decided to try and see Buddy McGurk at lunchtime. They figured that he would be unavailable on Friday when Green Ridge had an evening football game.

Buddy McGurk was in his office clicking through a catalog for football equipment. He really wanted to get some new football sleds, but they had gotten more expensive. Nonetheless, he would find a way to pay for them. Nothing was too good for the football team.

Sean Allen and Arthur Stewart appeared at the door. Buddy was not happy but forced a grin.

"Come in, come in!" he told the two captains. "Mr. Wimble says the practices are going well. I hear the first-year students are going to have a time-trial on Friday. Just remember that they must be off track by 5 PM. We must get things ready for the game in the evening."

"No problem, Mr. McGurk. We are here to talk about the season schedule," said Sean.

"Yes, there are no larger weekend meets until the league and county championships in late October. We really need to go to an invitational or two. Our runners need practice running in larger packs - especially our younger guys."

"I see," answered McGurk in a flat tone. "Well, I will be honest with you men. I will see what I can do but it will be tough. The budgets are tight this year. I will see if there is anything possible, but I am not promising anything. Thanks for stopping by. Now, if you will excuse me, I must take care of something immediately. You can let yourselves out."

With that, Buddy McGurk clicked back on the football catalog and started clicking to order the football sleds.

So much for the "A" in "TRACK," thought Artie.

On Friday, Artie returned home after school and cross-country practice. He was exhausted and collapsed on the sofa.

There was good news and bad news.

The good news was that practices were going well, and Ed Glavine looked to be a nice addition to the team. Ed was the best of the sophomores and had a chance at making the varsity seven. The first-year students looked good too. In their mile time trial, two of them ran under 5:15. They were Juan Alonso and Brad Benson who were both younger brothers of former teammates of his brother Ted.

The unwelcome news was that they had gotten nowhere with Buddy McGurk. Artie had talked about it on Thursday evening by phone with his brother who was now a first-year law student at State University. Ted said he had an idea but wanted to check it out first to see if it would work.

While Artie was mulling things over, his phone rang.

"Hi, this is Artie."

"Artie, it's Ted. I have someone on the line."

"Hi, Artie. This is Dave Toomey. I am the President of the Meadow Striders and a Green Ridge track alum. We met years ago when you competed in the Junior Olympics as a Strider. Anyway, I have been following your team on the social media page that Mrs. Mallory has set up. I was wondering about the skimpy schedule and spoke with Ted about it. We think we may be able to offer you help."

Artie immediately thought that the "C" for Communications to the Alumni in "TRACK" was paying dividends!

"I am all ears. Mr. Toomey."

"The deal is that the USATF State 5K Cross-Country Championship is two weeks from this Sunday at Near Path Park which is about 90 minutes away from Green Ridge. We already are entering one Open Men's team, but we could enter your team as a Striders "B" team. What would you think about that?"

"That sounds great. What do we have to do?"

"Not too much. The Striders will take care of most of the details but there are a few things."

"Go ahead."

"The High School Association has three rules about open competition. First, the school must approve. In other words, get your coach's okay. An email from him to us will do. Second, your coach cannot bring you to the open competition or coach you there. Third, you cannot wear your high school uniforms – but we will provide you with Strider shirts."

"That all sounds fine."

"A couple other things in the USATF rule book: All your runners must be sixteen years old on race day to run in an open championship race. And USATF allows eight runners on a team unlike high school and college which only allow seven on a team. You get to bring an extra guy! However, the places of the best five finishers still add up to the team score, just as in high school and college."

"How big a race does this expect to be?"

"Everybody goes off together at 10 AM: Open and Masters, Men and Women. We expect over 200 runners at the starting line. Is that big enough for you?"

"It certainly is! Should I email you the names of our runners?"

"Yes, their names and birthdates. The Striders will pay the entry fees – several Green Ridge alumni are chipping in – but we do need each of your team members to get their USATF membership current online if they are not already members this year from summer events."

"Will do. Thank you so much, Mr. Toomey. I cannot wait to tell the team. This may even be better than a high school invitational!"

After the phone call, Artie instantly sent a message to Sean and Tommy. They would get Mr. Wimble to send the email message on Monday. Things were looking up.

CHAPTER FIVE: MID SEPTEMBER

The second week of practices went well. On Saturday, Green Ridge had their warm-up scrimmage at County Park. The boys' team would face St. Joseph's high school, and the girls' team would face St. Mary's high school. This was a long-standing tradition.

Both the boys' and girls' teams from Green Ridge would be underdogs, but Artie was not particularly worried since the teams kept no scores in a scrimmage. He was more concerned about how the team was rounding out. Who would be the fourth and fifth runners on the varsity - and the sixth and seventh runners for that matter?

Artie, Tommy, and Sean were the top three runners on the squad, but they were quite different runners.

Artie was the closest to being a pure distance runner. He had stamina but not the speed of his older brother. He could push the pace in a race and lift, but he did not always have the finishing kick of his competitors.

Tommy was at home running the half mile during the track season. Cross Country was a bit longer than his comfort level, but he was a game competitor. In cross country, he preferred a slow pace leaving things to a kick at the end.

Sean had more stamina than Tommy and a better kick than Artie. He also happened to be one of the top young race walkers in the country. However, while the race walk is in the Olympics, it is not a standard high school event. Nevertheless, he could find opportunities to race walk outside the high school schedule.

After the top three on the squad, things were uncertain.

Artie was almost certain that Michael Thomas, the fourth senior on the squad, would not be among the top seven runners on the Green Ridge team. He always tried his best but was not really a distance runner. During the track seasons, he would stick to the 400 distance and nothing longer. Still, he contributed value to the cross-country group. He would be the unofficial captain of the junior varsity team, mentoring the younger runners, teaching them the finer points of the sport.

Of the four juniors, Frances Xavier and Dae-Sung Yu looked like the most likely to be on the varsity. Ken Zoller was also a possibility. Tim Wagner was a long shot.

Ed Glavine was the best of the eight sophs and Artie thought Ed had a real chance at making the varsity.

The scrimmage took place at County Park where all the Green Ridge meets would be until the State District meet at the Barrett Mountain course. They had the 11 AM to Noon timeslot which would include three races. The morning timeslot at County Park was fortunate because the day was already heating up and would be even warmer in the afternoon.

At 11 AM, the boys would start a combined varsity and junior varsity race that was 5 kilometers (3.1 miles) long. Ten minutes later, the girls would start a combined varsity and junior varsity race that was also 5 kilometers. Twenty minutes after that, the frosh boys and girls would start a combined race that was only 3 kilometers (1.9 miles) long.

Sean and Artie said hello to the top St. Joseph runners who were the twins Jim and John McCauley, and brothers Tony and Sal Nitto, all of whom they knew from prior years. They then went over to the starting line. Artie lined up next to Ed Glavine.

The starter's pistol fired its blank and the runners were off. During the first mile, six runners including three for each team - including Artie - formed a pack in the front. Thereafter, there were three more St. Joe runners plus Ed Glavine, behind the lead pack. The remaining runners trailed behind.

In the second mile, different runners tried to push the pace, but being the first race of the season, they were tentative in their efforts. Behind the lead pack, Ed Glavine struggled on the hills but made-up ground in between.

On the final mile, the lead pack broke into pairs. Sean outkicked Jim McCauley, but John McCauley outkicked Artie. Tommy outkicked both Nitto brothers, but the brothers and two more SJ runners were next before Frances Xavier, Chris Young, and Ed finished tenth through twelfth. There was no official score kept in a scrimmage, but by Artie's calculation, St. Joe's had a narrow unofficial victory.

A few minutes later, the junior varsity finished, and St. Joe's again had an unofficial edge, but later, Artie was pleased to see that Green Ridge dominated the frosh race. On the girls' side it was the same result, with Green Ridge unofficially losing both the varsity and junior varsity races but at least salvaging the frosh competition.

Four days later, the Green Ridge team returned to County Park for the beginning of the Northeastern Interscholastic League (NEIL) season. For five consecutive Wednesdays, Green Ridge would have dual meets or tri-meets against their seven league opponents at County Park.

Back in the days when his brother Ted ran, the NEIL meets were at home courses on high school grounds. Now, however, the meets were all held at County Park. This allowed runners to see if their times improved over the season and it prepared them for the league and county championships also held at County Park.

The NEIL created the league schedule, in part, by seeding the eight teams based on their performance during the preceding year. For many years, Riverside and Green Ridge had been the top two seeds (in either order), but Green Ridge was only seeded fourth this year.

The seeding was important for two reasons:

One reason was that when the Athletic Directors of the eight schools created the schedule months before the start of the season, and if there were any disagreements in setting up the schedule, the better seeded school usually got what it wanted.

A second reason was that in the final week of the league schedule always matched the closely seeded teams in showdowns like this:

Team # 1 against Team # 2

Team # 3 against Team # 4

Team # 5 against Team # 6

Team # 7 against Team # 8

In the recent past, this scheduling resulted in a showdown between Riverside and Green Ridge at the end of the schedule as the top two seeds. This season, Green Ridge would be an underdog against the top seeds.

The seedings looked like this:

1 Riverside

2 Meadow Regional

3 Overlook

4 Green Ridge

5 Spring Valley

6 Arcola

7 Eastwood

8 Undercliff

Artie hoped that the Green Ridge Knights could at least move up a spot to third place in the NEIL standings to improve their seeding next year. If the seedings were accurate, they would need to beat Overlook in the showdown at the end of the schedule. Either that or upset Riverside or Meadow Regional along the way.

In their opening meet, the Green Ridge Knights were facing the Meadow Larks, and the Undercliff Rockers. The tri-meet scored as if it were three dual meets: Meadow vs. Green Ridge; and Green Ridge vs. Undercliff; and Meadow vs. Undercliff.

As with the scrimmage, there would be three races in an hour timeslot. Varsity & junior varsity Boys, then varsity & junior varsity

Girls, and then combined frosh. This allowed NEIL to do a meet per hour allowing up to all eight NEIL teams to compete in an afternoon.

In a varsity & junior varsity race, the top seven finishers on each team constituted the varsity, and the remaining runners were the junior varsity. A team's score was the sum of the places of its best five finishers. The winning team was the team with the lower score. A team's sixth and seventh runner did not score directly but could cause an opposing team to have a worse score by finishing ahead of any of the opposing team's best five runners.

Green Ridge was an underdog against the Meadow team, but Artie had hope. In a dual meet, sometimes a strong trio of runners can carry a team. If Team A sweeps the top three places, it wins a dual meet as long as two other runners finish the race. Team A scores 29 (= 1 + 2 + 3 + 11 + 12) while Team B scores 30 (= 4 + 5 + 6 + 7 + 8). Sweeping the top three against Meadow, however, would be tough. The Green Ridge trio needed help from the rest of the team.

Artie did know that the top two runners on the Meadow team were kickers, more like half-milers than pure distance runners. Artie was not blessed with as many fast-twitch fibers in his legs as his brother Ted. He needed to avoid the race coming down to a frantic finish.

The Undercliff team did not expect to be much of a factor. They had little star power, and even less depth. In fact, they only had twelve runners stepping to the line, seven to score for the Varsity, and the bare minimum of five to score for the Junior Varsity.

The weather was nice, still a bit warm as expected in the early season, but a gentle breeze made it comfortable. The Varsity/JV race began and this time it settled into a lead pack of five runners: Sean, Artie, and Tommy plus the top two runners from the Meadow team. No Undercliff runners were in the top ten. Artie felt stronger than he had in the scrimmage and the pace was a bit quicker for the first mile this time.

In the second mile, Artie took the lead and pushed the pace trying to tire the Meadow runners out. But the Meadow runners did not fade and the pack of five hung together.

During the last mile Artie started a long drive toward the finish line but his legs were not up to it this early in the season. The four others pulled away from him. Sean outkicked the two Meadow runners, and Tommy (who was really a half-miler after all) sped by him too.

After Artie finished in fifth place, the next five runners were all from the Meadows team. Frances Xavier and Ed Glavine were eleventh and twelfth. The top Undercliff runner was thirteenth just ahead of Ken Zoller and Chris Young – the sixth and seventh Green Ridge runners.

The final score was the Meadow Larks 28 (= 3 +4 + 6 + 7 + 8) and the Green Ridge Knights 31 (= 1 + 2 + 5 + 11 + 12). On a happier note, Green Ridge came close to sweeping Undercliff by a score of 19-43. Meadow Larks swept Undercliff 15-50 by having seven finishers before the first Undercliff finish.

The JV team lost narrowly to Meadow but easily beat Undercliff. The frosh team did narrowly defeat Meadow and took the first five places over Undercliff to win by a rout. The Lady Knights split, losing the Varsity race but winning the JV and Frosh.

An upset would have been nice, but the split for the day would put Green Ridge in the middle of the NEIL Standings with a 1-1 record. Something to build on. They still had five more teams to face in the NEIL schedule.

When Artie got home, he sent the results to Mrs. Mallory to post on the team's social media page. He was keeping in mind the "C" for communication in "TRACK." The more the Alumni knew and got involved, the better.

CHAPTER SIX: LATE SEPTEMBER

*I*t was four days after the Opening NEIL meet and time to go to the USATF State 5K Cross Country Championships. Near-Path Park was about 90 minutes away from Green Ridge in a more rural part of the state. Huntington County was known for distance runners and often hosted significant races.

Artie had run on a 3K course at Near-Path Park years ago at a Junior Olympic meet. He recalled that the park had many rolling hills but fair courses that were also excellent for spectator viewing.

Artie knew a fair amount about USA Track & Field (USATF) both from Ted and his own experiences in Junior Olympics. In 1978, the U.S. Congress passed a law instructing the U.S. Olympic Committee (the USOC, and later the USOPC) to recognize a National Governing Body (NGB) for each Olympic sport. For track & field, long distance running and race walking, that NGB became what is now USATF.

USATF has a Junior Olympics program to introduce youngsters to the sport. High schools and colleges organize their own competitions but after that, USATF is responsible for adult competition in the USA and creating USA teams to compete in international competition all the way up to the Olympics. USATF also had 56 local affiliates (called "Associations") to foster local competition. Green Ridge was in a state with one of the largest Associations.

The USATF Rule Book allows eight runners on a cross-country team instead of seven. Sean and Artie needed to decide who should be the eighth runner on the team on Sunday. The Green Ridge varsity seven had sorted itself out: three seniors (Sean, Artie, and Tommy), and three juniors (Xavier, Young, and Zoller), and one soph (Glavine). They could have one more runner under USATF rules.

The captains decided to ask Michael Thomas to be the eighth man. He had never gotten to run varsity at a high school cross-country meet. This was the next closest thing. They also knew that he was unlikely to run cross-country for a college team next year. To extend his cross-country career, it would be with the Meadow Striders.

The race started at 10 AM which was a good thing because there was rain in the forecast for the afternoon. There was an overcast sky and gusts of wind, but the course was dry.

Soon after he arrived, Artie saw Ed Glavine with what looked to be his parents. Artie went over and introduced himself. Then he brought the Glavine parents over to his folks for more introductions. The parents started talking and Artie and Ed left to warm up and find Dave Toomey.

The Meadow Striders had a medium-size tent set up near the finish line. The boys found Dave Toomey and an assistant inside the tent.

Dave had the Strider shirts, bib numbers, and safety pins to attach the numbers to the front of the shirts. Dave warned them not to bend, fold, tear, or otherwise mutilate the numbers. Not only was it against every rulebook, but it also could harm the transponders on the back of the numbers which recorded each runner's time at the finish.

Dave filled them in on details about the race.

"It looks like there are eleven full teams in the Open Men's division. There are also a couple incomplete teams and individuals entered bringing the total entry to 103 runners. There are also about a hundred entries from the Open Women's division and both Masters divisions. The grand total is around 200 runners."

He continued, "The starting line has numbered paddocks marked off by chalk lines. The Striders have one team in each of the four divisions, plus your "B" team. Your team is in Paddock # 10, next to our Open Men's" A" team in Paddock # 9. Your top five runners are up front on the line, and your other three runners stand behind them."

Artie and Ed headed out of the tent and saw Sean. They started to jog on the course when two older runners in Strider shirts came over.

"Hi, you are Artie Stewart, aren't you?"

"Yes, I am"

"I'm Sal Alonso and this is Ken Benson," one of the runners replied. "We were teammates of your brother Ted. Our younger brothers are now on the frosh team. We run for the Striders now – on the "A" team today."

"That's cool."

"Anyway, we wanted to wish you luck. We have been following your team online and if there is anything we can do to help, just say the word."

"Thanks. I remember some of your races when I watched Ted's high school meets. I see that our team is right next to you on the starting line. I guess we will follow your lead."

"Great! We will see you at the start."

Artie, Sean, and Ed continued to warm up. Gradually they gathered their other five teammates and eventually headed to the starting line area. After stretching and striding, they were ready.

After the starter's pistol went off, the five top members of the Striders "A" team took off among the leaders. Artie knew he could not keep up with them, but he could stay close to the three trailing members of the "A" team.

As Artie settled in during the first mile, he could see that he was ahead of most of the master runners who were over forty years old. Among the runners in the Open Men's division, Artie seemed behind many of them, but ahead of at least a few of them. The good thing was that there were plenty of runners – in front and behind him, and in packs around him.

In the middle of the race, Artie tried to use the rolling hills to his advantage like surges to shake off opponents. The final kilometer was a long flat stretch and Artie tried to really work it. He passed several weary runners but was passed by a couple of kickers. He could see Sean finish ahead of him and Tommy came in only seconds after him. About a half minute later, Ed was their fourth man for the first time followed closely by Frances Xavier.

After the boys walked and jogged a little to cool off, they headed to the Strider tent and saw Dave Toomey. They had to wait until the posting of the official scoring, but he thought they may have finished as high as fifth or sixth place out of the eleven teams in the Open Men's division. The "A" team looked to finish second to the winning Huntington Harriers.

Sean and Artie assembled the entire "B" team, and they did a more serious jog to cool down. When they returned to the finish line area, the officials had posted the results. Sean, Artie, and Tommy finished 20th, 22nd, and 25th. The team had a score of 187 which placed sixth of the eleven teams.

Dave Toomey came by and spoke.

"Congratulations guys." he said. "Not too shabby against older competition."

"Thanks. It felt good to be in a bigger race," replied Artie.

"Now if you would like to run in a race against your own age group, The State Junior Olympics will be back here in early November if your high school season is over. If you qualify for the state high school meet, you can get a bye in the State Junior Olympics and go to the Regional Junior Olympics which is two weeks after the State meet."

He added, "By the way, this year, it is our state's turn to host the Regional Junior Olympics here at this park too. That meet qualifies into the National Junior Olympic meet which is in Florida in early December. Something to think about."

Sean and Artie thanked Mr. Toomey again and recorded the results to send to Mrs. Mallory to post online. This would be something good to tell the alumni – especially the ones that had donated to the Striders to pay their entry fees.

There was still another week in September.

On Wednesday, Green Ridge faced Arcola (#6) and Eastwood (#7) in another tri-meet. The competition proved less than anticipated as Green Ridge defeated Arcola 20-35, and Eastwood 22-33. The two teams seemed to have conceded the meet to Green Ridge and focused instead on the battle between themselves which Arcola won 26-29.

The Green Ridge boys' junior varsity and frosh teams, plus all three girls' teams also posted victories over both opposing teams.

CHAPTER SEVEN: EARLY OCTOBER

Wednesday, October 1st, was a big day. Josh Johnson was returning to Green Ridge High School to speak at the school. There was an assembly in the morning.

Coach Mallory had coached many fine athletes who went on to compete in college and beyond. However, Josh was the first one ever to be an Olympian. He had shocked nearly everyone except Coach Mallory and himself by finishing third in the 400-meter hurdles at the last Olympic Trials to make the USA Olympic Team.

Josh had a shoe contract with the Victoria brand. Victoria had dozens of track & field athletes under contract and to create good will (and good publicity), they started a program in which the athletes went back to their high schools and presented each school with a $5,000 gift card so the high school athletes could get Victoria gear. Artie was hoping for a new pair of racing shoes.

Artie was looking forward to seeing Josh Johnson. He knew him from when Josh was Ted's teammate. Josh had often handed off the baton to Ted in the 4x400 relay back in the day.

The boys track & field captains (Chuck, Bruce, and Artie) sat in chairs on the stage to the left of the podium, and the girls track & field captains (Debbie Novo, Terri Foster, and Valarie Price) sat in chairs on the right of the podium.

Suddenly, Josh Johnson bounced on to the stage and turned to Artie.

"Artie, my man," said Josh offering a fist bump. "I was afraid that I would not get to talk to you. They have me totally programmed most of today. This assembly, and then a workout on the track, lunch with faculty, and a press conference. But I set aside time to see your cross country race this afternoon. Tomorrow, I will travel. The 400-meter hurdle race is not an indoor track event, so I am going to Australia to train over the next months. When it is winter up here, it is summer down there. I will be back next March."

Principal Henson called things to order and introduced Josh Johnson. Josh went to the podium and addressed the assembly:

"Thank you for your warm welcome.

Superintendent Taft, Principal Henson, faculty members, coaches, students, and fellow athletes:

When asked to give a talk, they always tell me to keep it short. However, it occurs to me that the longer my talk is this morning, the shorter they will have to make the class periods for the rest of the day. We shall see if this will disappoint most of you in the audience.

(*Laughter*)

I plan to stay here at the school all day and accompany the cross-country team this afternoon to their meet to cheer them on. I even plan to have lunch with some of that excellent cafeteria food that I have missed all these years. The height of haute cuisine!

(*Laughter*)

But more seriously, I specifically asked that the six Green Ridge captains be up here on the stage with me.

On the boys' side, Artie Stewart is the younger brother of my best friend Ted. Bruce Griffin is a hurdler – always an excellent choice. And Chuck James is the best Javelin thrower that Green Ridge has ever seen. I hope when he finishes college that he can join me on the Victoria team!

On the girls' side, Debbie Novo is the best girl distance runner that Green Ridge has seen since Sue Evans back in my day. Terri Foster has a great name for a hurdler, and Valarie Price has a great name for a thrower!

Coming back to Green Ridge is a way to acknowledge my roots. My journey to becoming an Olympian began right here in this town.

First, it began as a Junior Olympian in the Meadow Striders youth program. My youth coaches Harold Wear and Vern Gale taught me how to hurdle and the basic rules of the sport. Most importantly, they taught me about sportsmanship and teamwork.

Next, I went to this high school and learned from the wise old fox himself, Coach Mallory. He helped me to become a state champion and taught me lessons which are too numerous to mention right now. I know he is currently in the fight of his life with cancer, and I look forward to visiting him tomorrow. But I want you to know that my four years here hold a special place in my heart.

My journey continued in college and after college with the help of more coaches who taught me the finer points of being an elite hurdler. When I went to the Olympic Trials, the commentators gave me little chance, but my coaches believed in me. I surprised nearly everybody by coming out of nowhere to make the team.

Now that I am an Olympian, my journey is not over. The next step is to seek to be an Olympic medalist. To do that, I first need to qualify to be on another Olympic Team at the next Olympic Trials.

And so, I am going to Australia to train in the coming months while it is summer down there.

The message I want to leave with you is that it takes thousands of people to create an Olympian. I would not have been on Team USA if I had not had years of competition against countless athletes along the way, at track & field meets which were possible thanks to the tireless efforts of numerous officials. And I would not have made it without my coaches at every level.

Our sport in this country is only secure if it has a solid foundation. Olympic athletes may be at the top of the pyramid, but our success depends on the rest of the pyramid being strong.

And what about the future? Who will be prospective Olympians in eight years, twelve, years, or sixteen years from now? That depends on our programs at the grassroots level producing athletes with potential. Think of it as a pipeline. If there are not enough athletes going through that pipeline now and in the future like in years past, then Team USA will be in real trouble in the Olympics down the road.

To help the effort, Victoria Shoes is presenting a $5,000 gift card towards athletic shoes and equipment to the high schools of each of its Olympic track & field athletes. We have a large-size replica of a gift card in front of the podium. I hope it helps Green Ridge!

Thank You!"

(Applause)

A photographer asked the six captains to stand on each side of Josh behind the gift card but in front of the podium. Next, Josh went over to talk to one of his old teachers. Then he headed to the locker room to change and do a workout on the track. Afterwards, he had lunch in the faculty room and talked to some more of his old teachers and to Mr. and Mrs. Wimble. Then it was to the library to read and catch up on messages until school was out when it was time to catch the team bus to County Park.

The Cross Country meet that afternoon was in moderate weather against Spring Valley. It was the fourth seed against the fifth seed in the NEIL. The Spring Valley team had Chris Speirs who had been all-county as a junior. However, they had less depth than Green Ridge.

In the end, it was a surprisingly easy Green Ridge victory. Spiers led the race from start to finish, but Sean, Artie, and Tommy were a pack behind him throughout the race to take the next three spots. Ed Glavine took seventh place and Frances Xavier ninth place to complete the Knights' scoring: The scorecard said Green Ridge 25 (= 2 + 3 + 4 +7 + 9) and Spring Valley 30 (= 1 + 5 + 6 + 8 + 10). Green Ridge lost to the boys' junior varsity, but the frosh boys won easily. The girls' varsity and frosh girls won but the junior varsity lost.

Josh Johnson wished Sean and Artie good luck on the rest of the season and until spring when he hoped to see them again – at the Philly Relays in April.

"Keep the faith!" were his parting words.

In the NEIL standings, the Green Ridge boys' varsity team was now in third place with a 4-1 record but would be an underdog in their remaining two dual meets against top-seeded Riverside, and third-seeded Overlook.

CHAPTER EIGHT: EARLY OCTOBER (CONTINUED)

October brought with it true autumn weather. There were still occasional mild days but more frequently there were brisk days with chilly wind. The earlier sunsets also made a difference.

Green Ridge had two more dual meets after which it would be on to the league, county, and district championships. But Artie was still unhappy that the varsity had had only one large meet (the USATF state championship) as a warmup to the larger meets upcoming.

Looking over the options, Sean and Artie noted that the Green Ridge 5K road race was on the Saturday between the last dual meet and the NEIL Championships. To be sure, it was on an asphalt surface instead of dirt and grass, but it would have hundreds of runners and it raised money for local charities. He penciled it in the schedule for a final team warmup for the championship season.

First, there was the dual meet with Riverside. Most years, the two teams were the top two seeds and would face each other in the final week. However, in the absence of Coach Mallory, Green Ridge had slipped and now Riverside was their penultimate opponent on the dual meet schedule.

Artie knew that this meet would be a much bigger challenge than the previous ones. And it was the first meet of the season run in chilly weather. Artie wore a Green Ridge ski cap.

As soon as the starter's pistol sounded, a pack of five from Riverside went to the front with Sean, Artie, and Tommy close behind.

The Riverside quintet knew exactly what they wanted to do. In the past meets, Artie often could set the pace, lead up the hills, and run surges. The Riverside runners did not let him do that, trading the lead and doing the pacing. Artie could stay with them but felt he was on the defensive, always reacting.

At 1.5 miles, the top two Riverside runners increased their pace. Sean was able to match it, but the trio gradually created a gap ahead of the remaining five runners in the lead including Artie. In the final mile, there were clearly two packs. The two lead runners for Riverside tried to shake Sean. He hung with them but was unable to pass either of them right to the end. Meanwhile, Artie tried to pull away from the next three Riverside runners. But try as he might, he could only do so to their fifth man. Their third and fourth men had kicks and finished ahead of him.

The pace had taken its toll on Tommy O'Leary's legs, and he did not have his usual kick and faded to seventh. Ed Glavine managed to take tenth place and Francis Xavier was eleventh. The final score was Riverside 22 (= 1 +3 + 4 + 6 + 8) and Green Ridge 35 (= 2 + 5 + 7 + 10 + 11)

The boys' junior varsity lost by an even more lopsided score of 19-40, but the frosh team behind a top two finish by Alonso and Benson eked out a 27-28 victory. The girls lost at all three levels.

The boys' loss to Riverside left Green Ridge and Overlook both with 4-2 records tied for third place in the NEIL standings with their showdown matchup the final week of the dual meet schedule.

CHAPTER NINE: MID OCTOBER

The meet against Overlook was in cool but dry weather. Artie could tell that the race was quite different from the previous week. He could control the pace again and he set it briskly over the first mile. Then Sean took over until the halfway point when they both put in a surge that pulled them away from the Overlook leaders. They did not look back the rest of the way until crossing the finish line and cheering on Tommy, Ed, and Francis to fifth, eighth and tenth place finishes resulting in a 26-29 victory.

The junior varsity lost to finish their season 4-3, while the frosh won easily to cap an undefeated season for the first time in a decade. The junior varsity did not go on to any championships. The boys' frosh team would run in frosh races at the league and county meets but not in the state meets.

All three of the girls' teams won to finish their dual meet seasons with winning records as well.

Now it was on to the championships. But first, the Green Ridge 5K served as a warmup with Coach Wimble's permission.

The 5K Road race was a big community event in Green Ridge. It raised thousands of dollars for local charities and had lots of local sponsors and volunteers. The mayor, council, police force and ambulance squad were all big supporters. It also received much publicity in the local press and media.

Once before, Artie had volunteered as a course umpire to support the town race when it did not conflict with the cross-country schedule. So, he was a bit familiar with it. He knew there would be hot shot local road runners, but he thought based on the expected times of top finishers that Sean, Tommy, and he had a chance to crack the top ten and win medals. Of course, if that happened and the leaders strung out early, it might limit their chance to do any pack running.

For the rest of the team, there would be an opportunity to run in packs and kick against plenty of opponents. This was important during the next few weeks. It was all because of something that Ted once explained that he studied in his Statistics course call the "Bell-Shaped Curve."

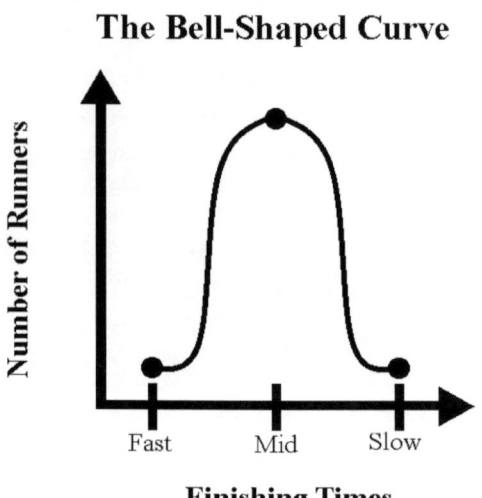

In charting the results of a large race and many other statistical populations, the curve on a statistical graph looks like a bell: at the beginning, it is low with only a few individuals; at the mid-point, it is high because there are many individuals in the middle, and at the end, it is low again because there are only a few individuals trailing. In short, the curve on the graph looks like a bell: high in the middle and low at both ends.

In cross country, in a dual meet which has only fourteen runners, the top three runners can sometimes carry a team even if the fourth and fifth men on the team are weak.

In a large race, however, the situation is different. The statistical results usually resemble a bell-shaped curve. Only a few runners reach the finish line in a fast time in the early going. Whether a team's top runner has a good or bad day may affect the scoring by only one or two points.

In the middle of a large race, there are a whole bunch of runners with middle range times – the top of the bell-shaped curve. Whether the fourth and fifth men on a team have good or bad day may cause a difference of many points.

At the end of the finish of a large race, there will usually be only a few trailing runners – often the sixth or seventh team members who do not directly affect the scoring.

In short, the fourth and fifth man can be the key to victory or defeat in a large race.

The emergence of Ed Glavine as a solid fourth runner on the team made things look more hopeful for the championship season than it had looked back in mid-summer. He and Frances Xavier were critical to how well Green Ridge would do in the big meets.

The Green Ridge team members went to the registration table together to pick up their bib numbers. Artie noticed that a flat and flexible timing transponder was adhered to the back of the number. The person at the table warned the boys not to bend, fold, or tear the bib number. Not only was it against the rulebook, and bad to the sponsor on the bib who helped make the race possible, it could also harm the transponder.

Artie pinned the bib number to the front of his shirt. Because it was against high school rules to wear a high school uniform in open competition, the boys were wearing their Striders shirts instead. This turned out to be useful.

The starting area had a crowd of several hundred entrants in the width of a street in row upon row. Pleasant weather had increased the turnout with last-minute entries. There were no paddocks at the starting line such as at some cross country meets with wider starting lines - just small signs along the side of the street with seed times suggesting which row to stand in the pack.

Artie noticed most local runners gave deference to the Striders shirts ("They must be serious runners!") and let the boys line up near the front on the starting line. Artie knew that there were good local road runners in the area but Sean, Tommy and he were hoping to be competitive.

The mayor started the race with an air horn. The start was an extended straight for two blocks before a 90-degree turn. The course was nice with shade trees - good since it was a sunny and mild day in October. There were turns throughout, but only a few hills. The course was not exceptionally fast or slow, but somewhat in between.

Artie noticed that volunteers were at every turn monitoring the course. Each volunteer had a large foam hand like the ones sold at stadiums to cheer on the home team. The volunteers used the foam hands to point the direction of the turns to the runners.

After a mile, the leaders strung out a bit. Sean and a runner in a dark blue shirt led the way, then two runners in red, then Artie and the rest.

Artie felt good during the second mile and passed a runner to move into fourth place. Then it was time to cross the town's famous one lane-bridge and into the final mile.

The bridge had existed for over a century. The area was originally farmland and the railroad wanted to lay railroad tracks through the town. Before giving permission, a farmer made the railroad company build the bridge so his cows could go from one side of his farm to the other. Now the bridge allowed runners to cross uninterrupted even if a train happened to be going by during the race.

In the last mile, Artie saw that the runner ahead of him seemed fatigued. He moved along side of him and then pulled away into third place. Up ahead, he could see Sean winning the race. Shortly after he finished the race, Tommy came up behind him finishing seventh.

Artie turned around and watched down the long straight to the finish line. The runners were now finishing in bunches. Ed Glavine was the next teammate headed toward the finish and Artie was pleased to see him outkick three other runners. Then came Frances Xavier whose kick was not as strong. He did outkick two runners but was outkicked by two others.

The team's sixth and seventh runners Chris Young and Ken Zoller were further behind.

After the race, Sean, Artie, and Tommy picked up their medals at the Awards Ceremony. A guy introduced himself as Tyler Ransom and struck up a conversation.

"How come you aren't at a high school cross country meet today?"

"Because our Athletic Director is too much of a cheapskate to enter us," quipped Artie before Sean or Tommy could say anything.

Artie knew the Daily Chronicle's sports staff by sight, especially Paul Grant who was their track & field and cross country correspondent. He did not know that Tyler Ransom was on the Daily Chronicle's staff for its features section and assigned to report on what was one of Green Ridge's big annual community events.

CHAPTER TEN: MID OCTOBER (CONTINUED)

On Monday morning, Green Ridge Principal Lyle Henson had a headache. He had seen the feature article in the Sunday Chronicle about the Green Ridge 5K. The picture of the top finishers receiving their awards had caught his attention because it included a couple of his students, Sean Allen, and Arthur Stewart.

The principal read the article and saw Arthur's quote about Buddy McGurk being a cheapskate. Shortly thereafter, he got a phone call from McGurk demanding that Green Ridge suspend Stewart from the Cross-Country team for insubordination.

What to do? The situation caught him in a bind.

On the one hand, McGurk had many supporters including certain members of the Board of Education. On the other hand, Mr. and Mrs. Stewart were respected members of the community who had helped the school on various occasions. Often, they gave guest lectures at the school, Mr. Stewart on economic topics, and Mrs. Stewart to the financial literacy classes about income taxes and accounting. The Stewart family would have their supporters too.

And why did young Stewart have to put his foot in his mouth? And why did this have to happen the week of the cross-country league championships?

Principal Henson decided the best course was to have an informal hearing and hoped that he could keep this from being a big issue. He decided to schedule it for Tuesday and told his secretary to notify the parties to meet in his office after school. McGurk could have his assistants oversee football practice for a while, and Stewart would have to be late for Cross-Country practice.

On Monday evening, Artie spoke to Ted and told him about the upcoming meeting on Tuesday.

"Can they really suspend me from the team?" asked Artie. "In History class, they said the First Amendment protects Freedom of Speech."

"The most recent case decided by the Supreme Court about a student's free speech was the Levy case in 2017. The school cut a student from the cheerleading squad and the student badmouthed the school on social media. The school tried to suspend her from school, and the Supreme Court said that they could not."

"That sounds pretty good."

"Yeah, but your case sounds different, McGurk only wants to kick you off the team, not suspend you from school. Note that the Supreme Court in the Levy case did not question the school's authority to cut Levy from the cheerleading squad. Also, keep in mind one other thing."

"What's that?"

"Court cases can drag on for years. In the meantime, this matter could mess up your entire senior year. Justice delayed would be justice denied. Our best bet is to try to resolve it favorably on Tuesday."

"OUR best bet? Does that mean you will try to help me?"

"Fortunately, I do not have any late classes on Tuesdays this semester. I think I can make the drive from the University to Green Ridge in time for the meeting."

"Great. Any advice in the meantime?"

"Yeah. Think about what you are going to say. Under no circumstances do you want to get angry or be nasty. Even if McGurk or anyone baits you."

"Okay. See you tomorrow."

On Tuesday afternoon, a group of seven assembled in Principal Henson's office: Mr. and Mrs. Stewart, Ted and Artie Stewart, Buddy McGurk, Principal Henson, and his secretary who was taking notes of the meeting.

Principal Henson saw Ted and spoke first.

"Why, Ted Stewart! Come on in. Josh Johnson told me that you are back at State University getting a law degree. As if already becoming a CPA like your mom is not enough!"

"Thank you, Principal Henson. It is good to visit the high school again."

"Well, each of you take a seat. This is informal today although Mrs. Jackson is taking notes to write minutes of this meeting."

"Let me start by passing around a copy of an article from the Living Section of the Sunday Chronicle. The article is about the Green Ridge 5K held on Saturday. In particular, three of our students finished in the top ten."

Everybody smiled except McGurk who continued to glower.

"Unfortunately, however, there is a quote from Arthur that they were running in the road race instead of a high school cross-country meet because Athletic Director McGurk is a cheapskate. Now, this not only puts Mr. McGurk in a bad light, but the school as well. We need to address this and decide what to do. But first, we want to hear Arthur's side of this and anything the Stewarts would like to add."

Arthur cleared his throat and began to speak.

"Principal Henson, I want to assure you that I did not know that the person with whom I was speaking was a reporter for the Chronicle. I know by sight the sports staff who cover track & field and cross-country for them. This guy was a new features writer. He must have been there because they consider the 5K a big community event especially due to its raising money for charity."

Ted spoke next.

"Principal Henson, we realize that Artie used a poor choice of words, but I suggest that truth should be a valid defense here. Artie and Sean went to Mr. McGurk before the beginning of the season and told him that the cross-country schedule was inadequate. The runners — especially the younger ones — need experience competing in larger races before the championship races later in the season. But Mr. McGurk did not change the schedule."

Mr. Stewart added:

"Speaking as an economist, I can tell you the marginal cost of adding a couple of invitational meets to the schedule is comparatively small. Most of the cross-country budget is for coaches' salaries and the uniform shirts. The athletes even wear their own gym shorts. There is little equipment expense unlike certain other sports such as football."

"I take offense to that," bellowed McGurk. I spend countless hours working on athletic budgets. I try to give every sport what it needs."

"I'd be willing to offer my accounting and auditing services free of charge to analyze the athletic budgets in detail'" responded Mrs. Stewart.

The look on Buddy McGurk's face made it clear that he did not like that idea.

"I appreciate the offer, Mrs. Stewart," answered Principal Henson. "But I am sure that the CPA firm we already use can provide us with anything we need. Coach McGurk, would you like to say anything?"

"You bet that I would. I spend hours and hours looking at the Athletic Department's budgetary numbers. All our teams would like to increase their budgets. There are never enough funds to give everybody what they want. I must use my best judgment to make the tough calls."

Buddy McGurk paused for a moment and then continued.

"I also do not appreciate a malcontent ridiculing me in public. It is insubordination, pure and simple. If Stewart wants to compete in outside competition such as the Green Ridge 5K, I suggest he do it full time, and skip the opportunities in cross country that the high school is trying to give him."

Just then, there was a knock on the door. In walked Sean Allen and the girls' cross-country captain, Debbie Nova.

"Do you two have something you would like to say about all this?' asked the principal.

"Yes," said Sean. "We took a vote and the boys' team will all quit if Artie is not allowed to finish the season as our Co-Captain."

"And the girls' team voted and is in agreement and we will all quit as well," added Debbie.

Artie was horrified. This would play right into McGurk's hands. He would be fine with there being no more cross-country teams.

"Please, Mr. Henson, I am sorry I ever spoke the words. I did not intend to put the school in a bad light."

Principal Henson was looking for something that he could consider as an apology and seized on the opportunity.

"Arthur, it takes a big person to apologize. I hope you have learned to be careful about what you say in the future, and we do not have any more incidents. I am taking that into account. However, I still think there should be a punishment and I am giving you detention this Friday. It is the day before the league meet so the team will be resting with no practice. The detention will not go on your permanent record."

"Thank you, Principal Henson," said a relieved Artie.

"Any other comments?" asked the principal.

McGurk was still unhappy but said nothing. He had made his point and figured that Stewart would not criticize him in public again.

"By the way," added Principal Henson. "It is too late to do anything about the schedule this season, but in the future, please talk to me first instead of making any other issues public. Okay?"

"Okay."

"We will adjourn so Artie, Sean, and Debbie can get to practice."

The Stewart family reconvened in the hallway.

"That was just a slap on the wrist," said Mr. Stewart. "It provides face-saving for Buddy McGurk, but little else. The important thing is that Arthur can complete the season as cross-country co-captain."

"Thank you all for helping me." said Arthur.

"Ted, can you stay for dinner?" asked Mrs. Stewart.

"I would love to, Mom, but I have an early class in the morning and exams are not that far away. I had better be getting back to law school."

The family divided up with Artie going to practice, Mr. and Mrs. Stewart heading back to their offices, and Ted returning to State University.

As Artie headed to practice, he saw Debbie.

"Thanks a bunch, Debbie," he said.

"If you really want to thank me, you could take me out to a movie this Saturday," Debbie said coyly.

"You got it." answered Artie with a smile.

Artie was not yet ready for a steady girlfriend and wanted to play the field for a while. But an evening out with Debbie would be enjoyable anytime.

CHAPTER ELEVEN: LATE OCTOBER

During the rest of the week following the meeting in Principal Henson's office, the cross-country practices shifted a bit. There was less mileage, more speed, and simulated kicking as the team was trying to peak as they headed into the championship weeks of the season. The junior varsity season had finished but Tim Wagner and Michael Thomas continued practicing with the seven varsity runners in case any of the varsity became sick or injured.

On Saturday morning, the team assembled at County Park. There were 56 runners in the Varsity Boys race – seven from each of the eight teams in the NEIL.

Green Ridge had finished third in the dual/tri standings but needed to match it and finish third in the league meet to improve the seed for Green Ridge next year from fourth to third. If they upset Riverside or Meadow Regional and finished better than third in the meet, they could even end up with a better seed, but if they finished fourth or worse in the meet, their seed could drop below third.

Artie knew the key to the meet was at a minimum to beat Overlook again to clinch third place. It might be tougher to beat them than in the dual meet. The Bell-Shaped Curve could work against them in the larger meet if their fourth and fifth runners did not have good days.

The league meet was in exceptionally mild weather for October. Soon after the race began, a pack of fifteen runners developed at the front: five from Riverside, three from Meadow Regional, three from Overlook, Sean, Artie, Tommy, and Chris Spiers from Spring Valley.

After a mile, the pack split into two smaller parks with two Riverside runners, a Meadow runner, an Overlook runner, and Tommy falling back into a secondary pack of five.

Chris Spiers soon pushed the pace and a gap formed between him and the rest of the field. Two Riverside runners, a Meadow Lark, and Sean formed the first pack behind Spiers, while the remaining five including Artie formed a secondary pack.

During the second mile, Spiers increasingly pulled away from the field, the two Riverside runners led the following pack, and Artie tried to push the pace of the secondary pack but could not shake any of the others.

During the final mile, Spiers increased his lead to win by about a hundred meters and the Riverside runners finished second and third. The top Meadows runner outkicked Sean for fourth. Artie could only outkick one Overlook runner in the secondary pack to finish ninth. Tommy finished twelfth about ten seconds later. Ed Glavine cracked the top twenty with a nineteenth-place finish by pulling ahead of another Overlook runner in the final meters.

The boys waited until they saw Francis Xavier finish in 30th place. Then they held their collective breaths until the scorer posted the results. It was close for third place among the teams. Riverside won easily with a score of 38 (=2 + 3 +7 + 11 + 15), followed by Meadow Regional with 63 (=4 + 8 +13 + 17 + 21), and Green Ridge at 75 (=5 +9 + 12 + 19 + 30) just ahead of Overlook at 76 (= 6 +10 + 14 + 20 + 26). The other teams were over a hundred, including Undercliff last with a 232 score.

The Green Ridge boys' team went over to pick up their bronze medals and a small third-place plaque that would go into the school trophy case. It was nice finally for the team to get a piece of hardware this year. Green Ridge's seed in the league would improve by one place in cross-country next season. And they had matched the Green Ridge girls' team which had also finished third in the meet.

Artie also noticed that Sean, Tommy, and he all had times under 17 minutes - a first. Times vary on different cross-country courses. For the Country Park course, it was a notable achievement to make the "sixteen-something" list.

CHAPTER TWELVE: EARLY NOVEMBER

Next up were the County Championships after another week of training – more tapering to peak for the championship season. In other words, less mileage, and more speed.

The number of athletes on the starting line in the County meet was almost double the size in the league meet – over a hundred runners. All the NEIL teams were in Class 3A but the biggest schools in Class 4A were with them in the Large Schools race. Nevertheless, the NEIL schools had a history of holding the edge in County competition.

Artie realized that this was his last high school race at County Park and vowed to make it a good one as he headed to the line.

A cold snap had hit the area and the boys waited until the last seconds to remove their sweatsuits before the race. They handed the sweatsuits over to Tim Wagner and Michael Taylor who were the alternates on the varsity team.

Against the stiffer competition, Chris Spiers did not wait and immediately took the lead with a stiff pace. His action started a reaction and the top group in the field strung out more quickly than usual. Artie found himself in about twentieth place at the mile but worked the middle part of the race to pass two runners.

In the final part of the race, Artie found that the early pace by Spiers had taken the starch out of the nearby runners' legs, and they did not have their usual kicks. Nobody passed him and he was able to overtake three more runners (including one from Overlook) just before the finish line.

The meet used chip timing with the "chips" adhered on the back of the bib numbers. Thus, long multiple chutes were unnecessary to funnel the runners and keep them in order as used to be the case in the "old" days when Artie's brother Ted was running in high school. Artie walked to the exit of the finish line area. He soon learned that he had finished in fifteenth place.

Artie saw that Tommy and Ed had finished behind him, but Francis Xavier was nowhere in sight. Finally, Chris Young crossed the finish line as the fifth man for Green Ridge.

What had happened to Xavier? Eventually, they all found out. He had tripped and taken a bad fall at about the two-mile mark. He had hurt his ankle badly. A Park Ranger on a golf cart saw him limping badly and gave him a lift to the finish area. He was going to have to go to the hospital for x-rays of his ankle.

Artie and his teammates went over to Mr. Wimble. He had written their unofficial places on a pad on his clipboard: Sean had finished seventh, Artie was fifteenth, Tommy was twentieth, and Ed was 28th. Chris Young finished all the way back in 50th place giving Green Ridge a total of 120 points.

Mr. Wimble went over to the results area. Coaches and runners from various teams anxiously waited for the posting of the results. It turned out that Riverside defended its championship title edging Fairmont (a Class 4A school) by a score of 57 to 66. Park Valley (another 4A team) narrowly defeated Meadow Regional 74-76 for third place.

With the posting of the scoring details, Artie saw that each of Green Ridge's first four runners finished ahead of the corresponding Overlook runners by one or two places. However, the fifth Overlook runner finished sixteen places ahead of Chris Young to make them the fifth-place team over Green Ridge by a 112-120 score.

The Green Ridge team jogged to cool down and watched the other races. The frosh boys' team helped by first and third place finishes by Alonso and Benson won the freshmen County team title to complete their season. The varsity girls finished eighth- and first-year girls finished fourth.

Watching the Small School (Classes 2A and Single A) race, Artie noted that only a few times in those races were faster than his time. He figured he had a good shot at third-team All-County or at least had clinched at least an honorable mention.

The boys finished their jog and said good-bye to County Park for the season.

CHAPTER THIRTEEN: EARLY NOVEMBER (CONTINUED)

Next on the November schedule came three Saturdays of state cross-country competition. However, only teams good enough to qualify would get to run on the second and third weekends.

On the first of the three weekends, four district meets took place around the state. Green Ridge belonged to the Northeast District which included teams from four counties. Their team would be competing only against Class 3A teams which were in a race that totaled about twenty 3A teams in the district.

In addition to the NEIL teams from Meadow County, they would be running against other teams from schools about the same size as Green Ridge from neighboring counties. They had not seen these teams all season thanks to their limited schedule. There were teams that they knew from past seasons such as Nuttersville, Clifford, Wynn Valley, Union Hill and Bayzone.

The top five teams and top ten individuals in their race would qualify for the State Classified Championships the following Saturday. At the State Classified Championships, the top five teams and top ten individuals in each Classification would qualify for the State All-Class Championships on the third Saturday which was on the weekend before Thanksgiving. It completed the in-state high school cross country season.

Artie knew that Green Ridge was a long shot to make it all the way to the All-Class meet, but he had had hopes of Green Ridge qualifying at least for the second weekend in the State Classified Championships. However, the possible loss of Frances Xavier dimmed those hopes. But never say never.

The Northeast District meet was at the Barrett Mountain course in neighboring River County. It was a tough course. Artie recalled his brother Ted (who was not much of a distance runner) dreading any meet at Barrett Mountain. But he saw the course as a worthy challenge. It started on a plateau and went downhill in segments with intervals of leveling. Then it bottomed out in the middle and reversed to go uphill during the return to the plateau and finish line.

In short, the course favored strength runners over kickers and that was simply fine with Artie Stewart. Of course, it would be the true test for Ed Glavine who had never seen a course like this in Florida.

Green Ridge had managed to stay healthy most of the season but during the week, they learned more unwelcome news on the health front. On Monday, they got the news on Frances Xavier. While the x-rays of his ankle showed no fracture, he did have a bad ankle sprain and his cross-country season was over. Dae-Sung Yoo, Ken Zoller, and Tim Wagner became the fifth, sixth, and seventh runners on the varsity for Green Ridge - but not for long.

On Thursday, two days before the County meet, Wagner called in to the school sick with the flu. And so, Michael Thomas moved up to the varsity as a replacement at what would be his final high school cross country meet.

Saturday's weather was cold, blustery, and included the first appearance of snow flurries during the fall season. Artie was wearing a light long sleeve shirt under his uniform as well as gloves and his school ski cap.

The starting line was marked off into paddocks for each team. Green Ridge had Paddock #12 near the middle of the starting line. Each team placed their top five on the line and their #6 and #7 runners standing behind them.

At the start of the race, Chris Spiers again took the early lead but this time there were other runners right at his heels. The pace was fast – particularly on the early downhills. Artie settled in at about thirtieth place. Sean was ahead of him but within Artie's sight.

Eventually, Artie reached the turn-around point and started to attack the uphill segments of the race. He began to make headway and passed some runners. He started a long drive to the finish before reaching the final plateau. The course had taken its toll on the potential kickers and Artie picked off some more runners ahead of him. With 200 meters to go, he even passed Sean. He finished in 20th place, two spots ahead of Sean.

Artie turned around to see Tommy struggle to finish 30th. About 30 seconds later, he saw Ed struggle even more to finish in 43rd place. It was a shame that Ed did not get a chance to run Barrett Mountain course at an early season invitational to prepare him better for the challenge today. Finally, Chris Young finished the scoring for Green Ridge with a 72nd place finish.

Green Ridge had a 187-team score. Artie was not sure if the score was good enough to earn fifth place in the team scoring. He was almost certain that Riverside, Meadow Regional, Clifford, and Union Hill had earned the top four places, but the scoring between Wynn Valley and Green Ridge appeared to be close.

Minutes later, word got out that Wynn Valley and Green Ridge had tied for fifth place. Artie frowned. He knew from two years ago that the tiebreaker in high school cross country is to compare the places of the sixth runner on each team. Two years ago, the Green Ridge JV had won such a tie breaker in a dual meet. He was less confident this time.

In a short while, the official results confirmed Artie's pessimism. The sixth man on the Wynn Valley team had beaten Ken Zoller by ten places. Wynn Valley won the tiebreaker and was the last Class 3A team at the district meet to qualify for the State Classified meet. Green Ridge's cross-country season at the state high school level had ended. The boys' team did not qualify to advance, and the girls' team did not qualify either.

CHAPTER FOURTEEN: EARLY NOVEMBER (STILL CONTINUED)

The boys now faced a situation that they had known was a possibility for weeks – especially after Francis Xavier had hurt his ankle. Their state high school season was over in early November. What to do the rest of the month?

There were three options.

Option One was to say goodbye to cross country and begin to train for winter track & field. Official practices with Mr. Wimble would not start until after Thanksgiving, but Bruce Griffin and Chuck Jones were already holding informal practices.

Artie did not like this option. They had spent months training for this point of the cross country season, and it seemed a shame not to race some more when they were at their peaks.

Option Two was to try to get Green Ridge entered in a Regional high school meet on Thanksgiving weekend which qualified teams for a national high school cross country championship.

This option was a non-starter for two reasons. First, Buddy McGurk would never approve it. Second, without a strong fifth runner, Green Ridge realistically had no shot at qualifying for the National meet. It hadn't even qualified for the state meets.

Option Three looked more promising. The USATF State Junior Olympic Cross Country Championships had 15 to 18-year olds as their oldest age division. They could run on a Striders team.

Artie and Sean had discussed this possibility with the McCauley twins and Nitto brothers from St. Joseph High School.

Next, they contacted Striders chief Dave Toomey and his assistant who quickly agreed to a Striders team consisting of Sean, Artie, Tommy, and Ed plus the St Joseph foursome. USATF rules allowed eight on a team, and they would be a solid group with a chance to advance. Five teams in each age group advanced from the state meet to the regional meet, and five teams from the regional meet to the national meet.

To beat the entry deadline, the Striders had entered a team even before the boys had run in the high school district meet. Dave indicated that their chances of advancing from the Junior Olympic state to regional meet were excellent. The younger age groups usually had big turnouts at the meet but the entry for the 15 to 18-year olds was usually modest. However, advancing from the regional meet to national meet would be a stiffer test.

The only drawback was that the Junior Olympic state meet was on Sunday, the day after the high school district meet. USATF rules provided that any runner whose high school season was not over could take a bye directly to the USATF regional meet, skipping the Junior Olympic state meet. However, since neither the boys' team from Green Ridge, nor St Joe's had qualified at the district meets, their high school seasons were over, and they needed to run the next day at the Junior Olympics.

The Junior Olympics state meet was back at Near Path Park and Artie was thankful that they had had the chance to run the course in September. It would be much colder this time. On the drive to Near Path Park, Artie noticed more snow flurries.

The schedule of Junior Olympic races started with the younger age groups during the morning and ended with the 15 to 18-year olds just after noontime. When Artie and the others arrived, the 11 & 12-year-olds were running. They went to the Striders tent near the finish line and checked in with Dave Toomey and his assistant who gave them their bib numbers and safety pins. He also gave Strider shirts to the St. Joe guys, but Sean, Artie, Tommy, and Ed already had their Striders shirts from September.

Artie could see that the younger races in progress were quite competitive with a good turnout. But Twomey told them that their race looked to have a light turnout – especially if some of the runners whose high school season was not over decided to take the bye into the Junior Olympic regional meet.

After Sean and Artie showed the McCauley twins and Nitto brothers key parts of the course on their warmup, the boys did stretch and stride, and it was close to time for their race.

Just then, there was an announcement for the runners in the 15 to 18-year old age group. Some entrants had qualified for next week's high school meet and accepted the bye into the Junior Olympic Regionals. As a result, there were only five boys' teams, four girls' teams, plus individuals (without teams) that had checked in. All told, there were about fifty boys and forty girls. They would all qualify and advance to the regionals if they merely finished the race and avoided disqualification for doing something foolish like cutting the course or interfering with another runner.

Since everyone should qualify, the meet organizers decided to start the boys and girls together to save time. Given the chilly weather, they also gave the runners the option of wearing their sweatsuits if they unzipped them at the finish line to show their bib numbers.

Since most entrants in the race had run the day before, there was general agreement among the runners at the starting line to take the pace easy. Treat the race as an easy workout until the end when anybody could kick if they wanted. Final places did not matter very much. Everybody would advance to the regional meet.

The eight Striders stuck together as a pack. At the start Artie felt a bit stiff and sore from the previous day but the relaxed pace allowed him to loosen up. When they got to the final stages of the race, the Striders felt good and lifted their pace. They finished strong in second place and won silver medals without even trying hard. Most importantly, they were going to the Junior Olympic Regional meet which would take place in two weeks.

CHAPTER FIFTEEN: MID NOVEMBER

*T*wo weeks later, the Regional Junior Olympic meet included runners from four states. The site rotated each year. This year, the Striders had home-course advantage as the meet was right back at Near Path Park giving teams that had been there for the Junior Olympic state meet an edge.

While there could be a maximum of twenty teams qualifying for their race, Sean and Artie had kept checking the entries online the week before and saw at the deadline there were twelve teams entered - four of the five qualifying teams from their state meet and eight other teams willing to make the trip from out-of-state. Artie recognized the names of some teams from other states. He had even run against some of them in his younger Junior Olympic days: the Keystone Klub, Flyers A.C., and Diamond T.C.

Once again, the schedule of races started with the younger age groups and would end with the 15 to 18-year old races. Their Strider team would run in the early afternoon.

Fortunately, the weather was much milder than two weeks earlier: cool but not cold, partly cloudy, and almost no wind. Close to perfect running weather.

The twelve teams plus individual runners went to the line – about a hundred runners at the start. A couple of the Keystone runners and two Flyers took the lead, then a half dozen more runners, and then a pack of five Striders: the McCauley twins, Sean, Artie, and Tommy sticking together in the early going along with three other runners hanging with them. Meanwhile, Ed Glavine and the Nitto brothers were in a secondary pack not too far behind.

The teammates in the Strider pack took turns leading the group. Artie felt good with the pace. The rolling hills were an opportunity, not a problem. They could exact a toll on the opposing runners. During the second mile, the Strider pack picked off two runners that had been ahead of them.

With a mile to go, Artie started his long drive to the finish line. The others went with him. With a half mile to go, it became a free-for-all. Sean and Jim McCauley went by Artie, but he passed two Flyers who were fading while no one passed him. Still, the Strider pack stayed close together.

In the team scoring, Sean was in fourth, Jim McCauley was eighth, Artie ninth, John McCauley eleventh, and Tommy twelfth. That added up to a 44 score. While other teams had two or three runners in the top ten, none of them had a fifth runner in the top fifteen. In fact, Ed Glavine kicked past two runners in the final 100 meters to take the eighteenth spot and displace the fifth runners on other teams. When the scoring was final, it confirmed that the Strider team had led all the other teams. They had won the gold medals and qualified for the Nationals which would be in Florida in early December!

CHAPTER SIXTEEN: LATE NOVEMBER

*E*ven though there were three weeks until the National Junior Olympics, there was much to decide quickly.

The first order of business was to determine if all eight of the boys on the team could go to the National meet in Tallahassee, Florida. The Striders would pay for the entry fees and provide $100 per runner towards the travel – thanks to donations. The families must absorb the rest of the travel costs.

Things fell into place to make a trip to Florida possible.

For starters, Ed Glavine's grandparents lived just outside Tallahassee, FL. They offered to put up all eight boys plus Ed's parents for the weekend. Next, the McCauley parents offered to drive the four St. Joe's runners to Florida in their minivan. Meanwhile, Tommy's dad, who did much business travel, offered to cash-in his airline miles for free tickets so that he and Mrs. O'Leary could take Tommy to Florida. Finally, Sean and Artie's parents told them that the trip would be an early Christmas present – one of Artie's best Christmas presents ever.

Next the team had to plan workouts to peak for the Junior Olympic race. On Thanksgiving weekend and the next weekend, they planned that all eight runners would train together. On weekdays, they would mix with track & field practices to do interval workouts or run the roads on other days.

Artie also had to plan with Bruce and Chuck the beginning of the winter track & field season even if he would not join the workouts until the Junior Olympic cross-country meet was over. The captains reviewed their T-R-A-C-K checklist:

T was for Training. Ted had already given Artie suggested workouts for the 400 & 800-meter runners. Other Green Ridge Alumni had submitted workouts for other events.

R was for Recruitment. The winter squad was smaller than past years but still had some blue-chip athletes. Team members were looking for potential new members – especially in gym class.

A had been to have an appointment with Buddy McGurk. Given what had happened in the fall, the captains agreed to change the "A" to Avoidance of McGurk. Talking to him was a waste of time. If things got out of hand, they would go to Principal Henson.

C was for Communication. The captains were submitting an indoor preview to Mrs. Mallory to put on the team's social media page. They had gotten good cross country coverage.

K was for Kilometers. Once Artie and his cohorts finished their peaking for the race in Florida, they needed to build a mileage base for the indoor track season. The rest of December (including winter break) would be a suitable time to do it.

On Thanksgiving, the Stewart family assembled to have dinner together and give thanks. Ted was home from law school and Artie filled him in with the latest update. Margaret was also home from college. Artie realized there was much for which to be grateful. In certain ways, the cross country season had turned out to be better than anticipated.

CHAPTER SEVENTEEN: EARLY DECEMBER

During the week after Thanksgiving, Artie, Sean, Tommy, and Ed continued to train for the national cross country meet. Everyone else on the winter track & field squad was training for the upcoming indoor season.

The track & field captains had created a set of workouts – with help from alumni (especially in the field events). Mr. Wimble approved all the workouts.

The first week and beginning of the second week went well. On the second Wednesday, Artie and Ed ran before school. After school, Artie, his parents, and Ed Glavine headed to northern Virginia to stay over with Mrs. Stewart's older sister before catching the Auto Train on Thursday. Ed Glavine's dad could not get away from business commitments until late afternoon on Friday, so Ed's parents would fly down to Florida to catch up.

Artie welcomed the chance to see Aunt Lynne who was his Godmother. Everyone got a good night's sleep and a substantial breakfast the next morning after Artie and Ed did a couple easy miles – purely maintenance at this point.

In the early afternoon, Mr. Stewart drove the foursome to the train station after a light lunch. They turned over the automobile to the handlers who would load it onto one of the special railroad cars that would take it all the way to Florida. Next, after waiting in the train station, they boarded the passenger section of the train.

Mr. and Mrs. Stewart had a full-size room – about seven feet by seven feet. By day, it had a sofa and cushioned chair plus a small bathroom and sink. In the evening, the attendant pulled down a Murphy bed.

Artie and Ed shared a "roomette" which was about seven feet by four feet. By day, it had two cushioned seats facing each other. In the evening, the seats converted to a bunkbed. The unit did not have a private bathroom. Instead, they used the restroom at the end of the railroad car.

First, Artie and Ed did school assignments they had to make up for the missed school. At 6 PM, they joined Artie's parents to go to the dining car for dinner. They had a reservation and a waiter promptly seated them.

After ordering beverages, the meal started with a salad, then the entrees. The boys had the pasta entree while Mr. and Mrs. Stewart chose the salmon. For dessert, everyone had cheesecake except Mrs. Stewart who chose the angel food cake.

Upon returning to their roomette, Artie and Ed found that the attendant had put down the bunk bed. They flipped a coin and Artie got the lower berth. However, the boys found it uncomfortable to study on the bunkbed, so they took their schoolwork and smart phones to the lounge car.

Upon sitting down in the lounge, Artie checked for messages on his phone and found that Sean and Tommy's plane had landed in Tallahassee. The St. Joe's contingent had stopped in Georgia for the night and would finish their drive on Friday morning.

Artie and Ed worked on their school assignments and finished early. They headed back to the roomette to call it a night. After visiting the restroom, washing up, and brushing their teeth, they returned to the roomette and closed the curtain to the window of the roomette. They checked their smartphones for messages for a while, set the alarms to wake up for breakfast, and then went to bed. The train made a slight rocking motion and both Artie and Ed fell asleep quickly.

Artie awoke the next morning refreshed and ready to go. He and Ed headed down to the dining car for a continental breakfast: cereal and milk, coffee cake, bananas, egg sandwiches, coffee, tea, and hot chocolate. Afterwards, they returned to the roomette and packed. The attendant came by with instructions for disembarking when they reached the train station. Mr. Stewart had given Artie money for a tip and Artie gave it to the attendant who thanked him.

The train arrived early in Sanford, Florida which was good because time was of the essence. Mr. Stewart had paid extra for priority departure and the attendants unloaded their automobile quickly and the Stewarts and Ed were on their way. They needed to travel about 200 miles north to arrive in Tallahassee by 2 PM for the guided walk around the course. The rest of the Strider team would already be there and waiting for them.

Fortunately, the weather was nice, and the traffic was light. Artie knew that Tallahassee was the state capital and the location of Florida State University but not much else about it.

They arrived at the course just as the course walk was beginning. Ed had never run on the course, but his grandfather had taken him to see a couple of national championships that had been there. The distances for those championships, however, were longer than the 5K that the boys would be running on Saturday. One thing that Ed knew was that most of the course was flat, but it did have one artificially created hill known as "The Wall." He was curious to run up it after all the training he had had on hills during the season.

The course was beautiful, and an official promised them that there would be no alligators in the vicinity! Artie was impressed and could understand why the course had served as the site for many championships such as the World and NCAA meets as well as the Junior Olympics.

Their course was a modified double loop. It began straight on grass and dirt almost a kilometer, then a left turn and eventually into woods at which the path was on crushed seashells which felt like crushed stones. The course continued counterclockwise and near the end of the first loop, there was "The Wall." It was not the biggest hill that Artie had ever seen but it was challenging. Artie was pleased that the course was not completely flat. Artie pointed to his teammates a mark about fifty meters before the hill.

Shortly after the hill, the course went left and into a second loop. With less than a half mile to go, the course came upon the hill a second time, then made a left again and a straight on which to kick to the finish, first on flat ground and then a downgrade the last couple hundred meters.

After the course walk, the team headed over to the registration table at which they found Dave Toomey and a Strider youth coach who had already picked up the Striders' packet.

Dave had a little sunburn and explained that he had been in Florida over a week. His company had a "use it or lose it" vacation policy and he had a bunch of vacation days left to use after Thanksgiving. First, he attended the USATF National Annual Meeting in Orlando. It was an important weekend at which he was a state delegate. He voted in elections, and on changes to the USATF Rulebook, on future championship sites, awards, and other matters.

Since Dave was already in Florida, he decided to use some more vacation days by staying in Florida until the Junior Olympic meet the next weekend. His wife came down and they went to St. Augustine for several days after the USATF meetings until the Junior Olympics.

Dave told the team that there were also a couple more Strider teams entered in younger age-groups. He gave the eight boys their bib numbers and safety pins. Then they talked about the race.

Dave confirmed what Artie had seen online. There were fifteen teams entered in the Boys 15 to 18-year old age group. That amounted to 120 runners. However, there were an additional 50 runners in the race entered individually. Since these runners were not part of a full team, they did not count in the team scoring under the rules. However, they would cause a more crowded start.

Most importantly, the top two teams from the past year had not traveled to the meet which was on the east coast for the first time in a while. The race looked to be wide open. Dave said it should take a score under 100 points to win the race.

The team went off to do easy jogging and stretching and then headed out.

Mr. and Mrs. Stewart had to stop first at their hotel to register and get their room. Then they headed with Artie and Ed to the home of the Glavine grandparents. The others had already gotten there except for Ed's parents who would be coming from the airport later.

The Stewarts introduced themselves to Ed's grandparents. Ed's grandfather was a retired captain for the State Police and had served at their state headquarters. His grandmother was also retired and had served as a nursing supervisor at a major hospital.

The home was nice and had memorabilia and plenty of family pictures. There was even a picture of Ed's grandfather running when he was a teenager.

Ed's grandfather began firing up the barbeque and his grandmother set the tables on the backyard patio for dinner. Ed's parents arrived from the airport just in time for dinner.

The meal was excellent: fruit salad (including Florida citrus), chicken, hamburgers, and fish, and key lime pie for dessert.

After dinner, Artie's parents headed to their hotel. Next, Ed's grandparents discussed arrangements with their guests. Their home had two guest rooms. Ed's parents would stay in one of those guest rooms. The other guest room would accommodate four boys: two on twin beds and two on cots. The other four boys would sleep in the living room: one on the sofa, one on the reclining chair, and two in sleeping bags. The boys picked numbers out of a hat and Artie won the spot on the sofa.

The boys played games on the home computer and smartphones and took a final look at the entries in their race. From what they could see, the big high school stars had chosen to go to the national high school meets instead, but there were still solid entries in Tallahassee. Artie recognized team names from his younger days in the Junior Olympics. It looked to be a competitive race.

The boys talked for a while before going to bed. As strategy for the next day, Artie suggested they make use of the hill by starting a surge at the mark fifty meters before the hill. They might catch opposing runners off-guard as they subconsciously braced themselves before the hill.

The discussion ended and the boys headed for bed. Once again, Artie fell asleep quickly.

CHAPTER EIGHTEEN: EARLY DECEMBER (CONTINUED)

Artie slept late on Saturday morning. The cross country races began at 9 AM, but the 15 to 18-year-old boys were the last race on the schedule at 3 PM. Artie ate a light breakfast. He had learned from brother Ted not to overeat before the race. Rice cereal with skim milk and apple juice would digest easily before race time and keep his stomach in order.

Eventually, the team, parents, and Ed's grandparents all headed to the course. The temperature was in the low seventies. It felt like late September weather back home. After they arrived at the site, the boys did a warm-up including brief stretching until they heard the call to the line.

The starting line did have paddocks chalked off and the Striders had the 15th paddock. Artie could see that there were teams from all over the country – even a couple from the west coast. They had to line up with five on the line and three in back. Sean, Tommy, the McCauley twins, and he were in the front. There were also the individual runners (who did not belong on a complete team) on the line. Altogether, there were about a hundred-seventy runners at the start.

A shot from the starters' pistol went off but a runner immediately tripped and fell. The starter fired a second shot calling the runners back. The USATF rulebook allows a call-back in cross country on grass or dirt, but not in a road race with a hard surface because of safety considerations.

The runners lined up again, and the second attempt to start the race was successful.

Runners from teams on both sides of the Striders were out like a rocket. Artie found that Sean, Tommy, the McCauley twins, and he were stuck in a big pack behind the leaders with little room to advance during the first kilometer. The clock at the kilometer mark showed 3:30 when they passed in the top fifty.

During the second kilometer in the woods, the five Striders found room and began to move up as a pack. They hit the two-kilometer mark at 6:46 and were in the top forty.

The five-pack of Striders continued to stay together and started their surge before the hill picking off and passing more opposing runners. Artie did not recognize most of the uniform shirts of their opponents.

On the second loop, Sean started to pull away from the other four. The twins stayed within range, and Artie could keep them in sight and was also still passing runners. Tommy did not try to go with them and would rely on his half-miler kick at the end. Artie hit three kilometers in 10:08 and four kilometers in 13:32.

The last kilometer was a battle. There were runners all over the place passing and falling back. Sean had a good kick and was passing runners. The twins were passing more than being passed right up to the end. And the second time on the hill allowed Artie to catch a couple more runners before the finish. Artie saw his time was 16:53. Five seconds behind him, Tommy picked off a runner in the last ten meters.

Artie walked beyond the finish line and saw Dave with a clipboard. He had been counting off the places of the Striders runners: Sean (18th), the twins (22nd & 23rd), Artie (29th), and Tommy (35th). That added up to 123 points for a raw score, but that score would be lower when the scorekeeping eliminated the individual runners from the team scoring. How much lower was hard to say.

The boys jogged a couple of miles for a cool down. When they returned, the officials had posted the results. The Striders had a score of 90 (= 12 + 16 + 17 + 20 + 25). It was good enough for gold medals at the national meet! The Bay State Rollers finished second with 93 points, and the Michi Ganders were third with 97 points. The Striders were the only Top Five team without a star scoring in the top ten, but they were also the only team with a fifth runner scoring in the top twenty-five. In fact, Ed Glavine (35th Place) and the Nitto brothers (43rd & 52nd) finished ahead of some fourth and fifth runners of other teams to inflate opposing scores.

Dave Toomey came over and brought the team to a stage where there was a brief medal ceremony, and photographers taking pictures. The parents and grandparents came over and offered their congratulations. Winning a national championship was a big achievement and certainly made the trip seem worthwhile!

The boys jogged a bit more and then everyone left the site and headed back to the hotels or Ed Glavine's grandparents' house. Artie went with his parents to the hotel, so he could take a quick shower there instead of waiting in queue for a turn to shower at the grandparents' house. The group had booked a reservation at a causal restaurant at 6 PM.

Everyone rendezvoused at the restaurant and promptly sat at a big table. Mr. Stewart rose first and proposed a toast to Dave Toomey and the Striders for sponsoring the team to make the weekend possible. He also thanked Ed's grandparents for being such gracious hosts during the weekend.

Next, Dave Toomey got up and made a toast to the team for their efforts and winning the title. He read compliments that the boys had already received on the Striders' page on social media.

Finally, Ed Glavine's grandfather got up and said that it had always been a dream of his to see his grandson run in a national championship. Today, he could say that he had lived to see that dream.

Mrs. Stewart happened to be sitting next to Ed Glavine's grandmother at the table. She told Mrs. Stewart that the grandfather had been a top runner in high school, but their son had never taken up running. When Ed had started running in age-group competition, the grandfather was thrilled and taught and encouraged him.

Ed's grandmother also mentioned that they had been concerned about Ed and family moving to Green Ridge and a new high school with no existing friends. They really appreciated Artie taking Ed under his wing. Now, every time they spoke to Ed, all he would talk about was the team and his teammates. It had made the transition an easy one - even with all those hills up north!

Mrs. Stewart responded that Ed joining the team had been like a gift from heaven. She filled the grandmother in on Coach Mallory's absence due to cancer. The team needed more depth which Ed helped provide. Now it looked like he might be the best runner on the cross country team next year. And with an excellent frosh team becoming sophomores next year, Green Ridge had the potential of being a formidable team.

After finishing dinner with key lime pie – one of Mr. Stewart's favorite desserts – the group left the restaurant. Mr. and Mrs. Stewart headed back to the hotel while Artie went with the rest of the team to the Glavine home.

On Sunday, Mr. and Mrs. Stewart picked up Artie and they went to church to give thanks. Afterwards, Mr. and Mrs. Stewart dropped off Artie back at the Glavine homestead. Artie would fly home with Ed and his parents in order that he could be back in school on Monday.

Meanwhile, Mr. and Mrs. Stewart stayed behind to do a circuit around Florida visiting friends and relatives for a few days and enjoying the warm weather before catching the Auto Train to begin the journey home.

CHAPTER NINETEEN: MID DECEMBER

News about the National Junior Olympics created a buzz in the school on Monday. A student sportswriter for the *Guardian* (the online school newspaper) even interviewed Sean and Artie. After the school day, it was back to practice with the winter track & field season ahead of them.

Buddy McGurk had scheduled no indoor meets for the team until after the New Year. In the past, Coach Mallory had directed a Polar Bear meet outdoors in December to start the season. It was not much of a fundraiser with only a handful of visiting teams, but it did give everyone on the Green Ridge team a chance to compete for medals at a meet in the early season. Without Coach Mallory around, McGurk discontinued the meet.

Artie, Bruce, and Chuck put their heads together and produced a two-part plan.

First, they suggested to Mr. Wimble that the team have time trials after school on the Saturday before the holiday break - just to get each athlete a time from a race or a mark from a field event to start the season. Mr. Wimble agreed, and the captains put out a request to the alumni for volunteers. They quickly had lined up a starter, three timers, a recorder, and several field event officials to cover the high jump and shot put in the gym which would be available because the basketball team had an away game that day.

Second, they contacted the Striders again. The USATF "Association" in the state had a series of youth development meets at the Liberty City Armory during the winter. Just like cross-country, it drew bigger entries of younger runners, but it did have age-groups for athletes at the high school level.

The first USATF development meet was on the Sunday between Christmas and the New Year. Mr. Wimble did not plan on any official practices during the holiday break - he and Mrs. Wimble were going on a trip to the West Coast. But the captains could still call voluntary practices, and Mr. Wimble gave permission on an email to the captains for any team members to go compete as Striders at the development meet. They could hit the ground running into the New Year.

Not to get ahead of themselves, there was the matter of two weeks of training to prepare for the season before the time trials. The team split into training groups. Groups A and B were the sprinters and hurdlers led by Bruce Griffin. Group C were frosh sprinters/hurdlers. Groups D and E were the quarter milers and half milers led by Michael and Tommy. Group F were the frosh runners in the 400/800 events. Group G were the distance runners led by Artie and Sean. And Group H were the frosh distance runners led by Alonso and Benson.

Artie and Sean were able to plan and suggest to Mr. Wimble workouts for Groups G and H. They had also gotten suggested workouts from Ted for Groups D, E, and F, and from Josh Johnson for Groups A, B, and C. In the gymnasium, the shot putters had workouts from Steve Brody, who held the school record in that event, and the high jumpers had suggested workouts from Kevin Bell, another alum.

The early season workouts included many hard intervals. Artie was still getting enough mileage done which helped his aerobic conditioning, but the middle distance and distance runners also need anaerobic conditioning for track races – running with their muscles in oxygen debt, especially in the latter stages of a race.

Interval workouts break down a race distance into smaller components that can be at nearly race speed repeatedly during a workout to get muscles used to race conditions. *Doing ladders* or *doing quarters* are common versions. The ladders for the distance group could be a Mile, 1200, 800, 400 down the ladder with a lap recovery (walking/jogging) between the intervals, followed by a 400, 800, 1200, and Mile up the ladder to finish the interval workout. A workout of quarters consisted of doing ten or twelve 400-meter repeats with a 200- or 400-meter walk/jog recovery between the intervals.

A track & field work-out for an entire team is logistically difficult to coach alone. In sports such as basketball, a coach can focus on the team in one place during most of the practice - the basketball court. In other sports such as football, there are assistant coaches, each working during practice with separate groups of players who play different positions. But a track & field coach must divide attention in diverse ways during practice. And Mr. Wimble did not even have an assistant for the field events.

Bruce Griffin told Artie that Mr. Wimble also did not have a stopwatch to time the intervals in the workouts and did not know how to use one. Artie called Ted who knew just the person to call on the phone for help. Lee Bailey was a distinguished alum who was retired from his job and free on afternoons. Most other officials considered him the best timer with stopwatches among the track & field officials in the state. And he was a good starter too.

Mr. Bailey could come to the practices until after Christmas when he headed to Florida. He brought a starter's pistol (which shoots blanks) to help the sprinters and hurdlers practice their starts. The rest of the time, he was with Mr. Wimble at the finish line. He temporarily lent Mr. Wimble two stop watches and gave him a catalogue to purchase inexpensive (but accurate) stop watches which could do multiple split times and finish times.

At the starting/finish line, Mr. Wimble followed a Green Ridge custom established by Coach Mallory at practice. The groups did not wait for a whistle to start each interval. With Wimble's nod they ran into the starting line as if they were running a relay leg but without a baton. Mallory said that it improved the flow of the workout.

Mr. Bailey also showed Mr. Wimble the basics of using a stopwatch with a split function. He told Mr. Wimble that he should have two stopwatches at practice because Green Ridge had enough groups that there would be times when more than one group would be running intervals simultaneously. If it happened to occur when Mr. Bailey was helping the sprinters and hurdlers with their starts at the top of the straight-away, Mr. Wimble would be on his own.

Mr. Bailey and Mr. Wimble also decided that it would be too difficult for Mr. Wimble to record all the interval times for all the groups on paper on a clipboard. Instead, they would call out times to groups as they finished, and the team members would be responsible for recording the times in the training logs they were supposed to keep.

The weather cooperated – it was cold, and the runners wore layers including tights. But there was little precipitation during the couple of weeks. The track was dry and in decent shape.

As the days progressed, Artie could feel himself getting in better shape. No matter how much he ran on the roads, the training on the track improved his speed and dealing with oxygen debt. His teammates felt the same way. Things were upbeat.

Finally, it was time-trial day. The boys were starting at 10 AM. The girls would follow in the afternoon.

An experienced coaching staff would usually take care of a time-trial session without the assistance of track & field officials. However, with Mr. and Mrs. Wimble being very inexperienced, and with no assistant coaches, they needed help. Fortunately, Coach Mallory had always strongly encouraged team alumni to become certified officials. It had always helped for the Polar Bear Relays and the Green Ridge Spring Relays meet.

Some of the alumni who were certified officials who had done the Polar Bear meet in past Decembers came to the time-trial this year. Mr. Wimble was at the finish line with some of them, while Mrs. Wimble was inside with others for the field events in the gym. The presence of the officials made the day feel more like a real track & field meet than a mere intra-squad session.

Every track athlete was running only a single race. There would be no 55 meter dash or hurdles on an outdoor track, so the sprinters and some hurdlers would each run a 200-meter dash. There would also be the 400 meters, 800 meters, and a Mile but nothing longer. The distance runners would all run the Mile.

Artie could see that the alumni who were officiating were introducing themselves to Mr. Wimble and giving him some pointers about timing races. They suggested that he time alongside them to assess his accuracy.

The sprinters went first. The 200 meters was a half lap on the outdoor track. It started at the beginning of the far turn on the other side of the track. It was good for the sprinters to try this distance because during the indoor season, some of them would be running in the 4x200 relay.

The Green Ridge track had six lanes and each section of the 200 meters had sprinters assigned to separate staggered lanes. After each race, the three timers got together and compared times. Even though the stopwatches show hundredths of a second, the rule with stopwatch times is to round up to the next tenth of a second because hand-timing is no more accurate than tenths. Fully Automatic Timing (FAT) uses hundredths of a second because it is more accurate - done with cameras and computers at larger meets.

Sometimes the stopwatches all have the same time when rounded to the next higher tenth of a second. In such cases, it becomes the official time. But sometimes, the stopwatches disagree in which case, the majority's time prevails. If all three timers disagree, the middle time prevails. And if there are four timers and they split two versus two, the slower time prevails.

The officials explained to Mr. Wimble, that human timers begin their stopwatches when they see the smoke of the starter's pistol, not the sound. This is because the speed of light is faster than the speed of sound. Officials can see the smoke quicker than they can hear the pistol go off. It makes even a greater difference when the starting and finish line are a far distance apart such as with the 100 meter and 200 meter dashes on a 400 meter outdoor track.

The officials also explained that the finish of a runner's race is when a runner's torso reached above the beginning of the finish line. The arms and legs do not matter.

They also told Mr. Wimble that even the best human reactions cannot duplicate Fully Automatic Timing. Therefore, in official results, stopwatch times are with the abbreviation HT (Hand-Timing), as compared to the more accurate Fully Automatic Timing (FAT). In comparing times from different meets, there is an accepted standard adjustment. An HT time requires an adjustment of 0.14 seconds slower to match a FAT time for races that start and finish at the same line, and an adjustment of 0.24 seconds slower in races that start and finish a distance apart.

Mr. Wimble could quickly see that these alumni, as certified officials, knew their stuff, and could give the recorder an accurate time for each runner in a race just moments after it was over. With each race, Mr. Wimble felt he was getting more of the hang of it and the times on his stopwatch were getting closer to those of the timers.

When the sprinters finished, the hurdlers ran next. Those that were candidates to run in 4x200 relays during the indoor season also ran the 200 meters. Others who would run the 400 meter hurdles in the spring ran the 400 meters with the quarter-milers. They might run in 4x400 relays in the indoor season. The quarter-milers all ran 400 meter races. It was one lap around the outdoor track with the runners staying in separate staggered lanes all the way around.

After the 400 meter races, the 800 meters was next. In major meets, the runners would have separate lanes for the first turn. But for a time-trial, they all just lined up on the curved starting line next to each other in one varsity race followed by one frosh race. Tommy led from start to finish and clocked a 2:00.9. He was a bit annoyed that it was not under two minutes and said that he should have taken it out faster on the first lap.

The final track event of the morning was the Mile. It was a long tradition in the state that a full mile (slightly over 1,609 meters) was the standard event instead of 1,600 meters. Coach Mallory had been one of the proponents for the Mile. It meant that the boys gathered at a curved starting line about nine meters behind the finish line to add the extra distance to four laps of 400 meters on the track.

Sean and Artie immediately took the lead with Ed behind them. Sean led the first lap, then Artie took the second and third lap. On the bell lap, Sean, as usual had the better kick and cruised to a time of 4:40. Artie was two seconds behind. Ed broke five minutes with four seconds to spare. They would all need to go much faster as the season progressed, but it was a start.

Afterwards, Mr. Wimble first thanked the volunteer officials. One of them handed him the results. He would post a copy in the locker room and give the captains a copy to give to Mrs. Mallory for social media.

Next, Mr. Wimble gathered all the runners on the team and wished them a happy holiday and noted that official practices would resume after the New Year when school was back in session. He encouraged everybody to stay in shape during the winter break while things would be in the hands of the captains. He and Mrs. Wimble would be away on the West Coast. He noted that the team's first indoor meet would be about two weeks into the New Year.

As the group headed inside to see how the high jumpers and shot putters were doing in the gym, Artie approached Mr. Wimble.

"Coach, we really wore through our training shoes during the cross country season and wondering about that $5,000 gift card that Victoria Shoes gave the school when Josh Johnson made his visit."

"You know, Artie, I was wondering about that myself. I asked Mr. McGurk about it last week. He said they needed to use all of it for football shoes before the playoffs last month. I know it is disappointing."

Yes, disappointing, thought Artie, but not a surprise.

CHAPTER TWENTY: HOLIDAYS

One wonderful thing about Christmas was that Ted was home from law school and Margaret was home from college. They had both finished their final exams for the semester and were home for the holidays on break before the next semester began in January.

Sue Evans was also home for the holidays only blocks away. Since ever Artie could remember, Sue and Ted had been a couple. At this point, she was almost like an older sister to him. Sue had been the best girl distance runner in Meadow County during high school. After an excellent college career, she joined an elite running team in the Pacific Northwest.

Ted was never much of a distance runner. But these days in law school, he was in no kind of shape to do anything beyond an easy jog with Sue. However, Artie was capable of being Sue's temporary running partner – at least in the first part of a workout. And it gave Sue a chance to catch up with Artie about the past season. She also hoped to catch up with Debbie to hear about the girls' team as well.

Artie related the major details about the cross country season. Sue congratulated him on the Striders team winning a national title. Artie also told Sue about their recent workouts for the winter season and Sue suggested a few tweaks.

On Christmas Eve, the Stewarts headed to the home of Uncle Angelo and Aunt Eileen, who was Mrs. Stewart's sister. Ted noted that being out of college, he was too old for all the adult females in Mrs. Stewart's extended family to pinch his face anymore, but Artie, still in high school, was fair game.

The presents (mostly gift cards lately) were nice, and the food was great. In his younger days, Artie would eat pizza, turning his nose at the seafood that his parents liked, but these days he had to agree with Ted that the lasagna was outstanding. Something to eat for carbo-loading! And the desserts were great too. Ted liked the cannoli, but Artie was partial to the spumoni and gelato.

The Stewarts headed home, and Artie went to bed. He no longer got up at dawn on Christmas morning but when everybody awakened, they headed downstairs to the Christmas tree. Artie opened his presents which consisted mostly of running gear. Mrs. Stewart had asked Ted exactly what Artie would like from Santa and he gave her promising ideas. Artie was quite pleased.

Meanwhile, Ted received a handsome attaché case with his initials (T.I.S.) inscribed on it. He would need it if he got a job as a summer associate at a law firm after next semester.

Next, the Stewart siblings gave their presents to the family. Experience had taught Artie that giving his dad socks was always a safe choice. And Ted had tipped him off that he should ask Mom what to give Margaret and ask Margaret what to give Mom. This year, it was scarves for both. Ted was more difficult, but Sue had suggested a legal book about Sports & the Law. Ted would be taking a seminar on the subject as an elective in the future.

After the exchange of gifts, Mom said it was time to go to church. The Stewart family arrived early because it was SRO on Christmas Day. Artie had a good voice, so he sang the Christmas carols with gusto. Artie knew that his mom was on the decorating committee at the church, and he had to admit the decorations in the church were spectacular. Mrs. Stewart beamed when he told her so.

Back home from church, Ted and Artie changed into their running gear and met Sue for a quick Christmas run. Artie wished Sue a Merry Christmas and off they went. Ted only ran the first couple miles, Artie went a few more miles, and Sue finished solo.

As soon as the brothers returned, they took quick showers and then it was fire drill time. The Stewarts were hosting a Christmas dinner for Mr. Stewart's extended family. Artie had learned to do any assigned chores pronto. By late afternoon, relatives started arriving.

Artie could not wait until his Uncle Jack arrived. Uncle Jack had been a star runner for Green Ridge in Coach Mallory's early years, and a track & field official in the years after high school and college. His own children, now grown, had taken up other sports. So, when Ted and Artie started Junior Olympic track, he was thrilled.

Uncle Jack had been following the reports about the cross-country season on social media and asked for all the details. He was a great cheerleader, encouraging Artie about the upcoming track & field season, and telling him not to let Buddy McGurk get him down.

On the previous Christmas, Uncle Jack had given Artie a subscription (electronic and print) to a national track & field magazine – as he had given Ted years earlier. This year, Uncle Jack gave Artie another interesting gift: a biography about Steve Prefontaine, plus two movies about him.

Artie had heard about Prefontaine, the great distance runner that tragically died in an accident when he was only twenty-four years old. Artie even knew that there was a track meet in Oregon named after Prefontaine, but he had no idea that there had been movies about him.

Before he left, Uncle Jack told Artie that he hoped to watch a few of Artie's upcoming meets. He also planned to officiate at the Green Ridge Relays in the spring.

CHAPTER TWENTY-ONE: HOLIDAYS (CONTINUED)

*T*he day after Christmas, Ted went with Artie to the voluntary team practice called by the captains. Ted timed the workout groups and gave some advice – especially to the quarter-milers and half-milers. The focus was on shorter intervals and speed before the meet on Sunday. The weather was mild allowing the runners to do a good workout. Meanwhile, the gym was open and a couple alumni helped the field event athletes set up for the shot put and high jump. Members of the girls' team also came to the workout.

Saturday was a day to rest. On Sunday, the USATF state development meet was at the Liberty City Armory. It was not a state-of-the-art Armory like the one that existed in a nearby state, but it served the purpose with a flat 200-meter track – half the size of an outdoor track. Ted told Artie that when Uncle Jack ran at the Armory, it was on a wood floor. Nowadays, it had a nice synthetic surface. At one end of the building, there were high jump and shotput venues.

The slate of events varied for each development meet. For this first meet of the season, there were a 55 meter hurdles, 55 meter dashes, 400 meter dashes, 1,500 meter runs, a 1,500 meter walk, and 4x200 and 4x800 meter relays.

Bruce Griffin was the only person from Green Ridge to triple in three events – the hurdles, high jump and 4x200 relay with three sophomores. Chuck James entered in the shot put. Tommy was running in the 400 meters, Sean was taking the opportunity to do a race walk, and Artie and Ed were going to run in the 1,500 meters. Sean, Ed, Artie, and Tommy also were doubling back to run the 4x800 relay which was the final event on the track.

Ted knew Dave Toomey who offered to help get times and marks for the team and get the Strider athletes checked-in for their events. This was particularly important for the younger runners on the Green Ridge squad. Some of them had never been to an indoor meet before.

With different divisions for boys and girls in six age groups (as young as the 7 & 8-year-olds), the meet moved slowly. It was all about giving athletes their first race or field event competition of the season and a time or mark to improve upon in the coming months. The entries in the younger age groups were heavy because they had fewer opportunities to run indoors. The 15 & 16- year-old and the 17- & 18-year-old entries were much more modest and mostly only one section per event per age-group.

Bruce and the three sophomores looked good in the hurdles. The sophs finished second, third and fifth in the 15 & 16-year-old race and Bruce beat his two opponents in the 17 & 18-year-old race with a time of 7.96. Dave told Ted that there usually the number of hurdlers at development meets was small. After he finished the hurdles, Bruce went over to the high jump and cleared 5'10" for third place. In the 55-meter dash, none of Artie's teammates scored.

Meanwhile, Chuck James was at the shot put venue. Until he could throw the javelin in the spring, this was his event. He preferred the outdoor shot put because it was a smaller iron ball that he could handle better. To prevent dents on the indoor floors, the indoor shot put was a larger sphere with a thick vinyl covering and buckshot inside it. He had a best throw of 52'6" for fourth place.

In the oval events, Tommy ran 52.92 in the 400 meters – good for a silver medal. He said he felt a little rusty and could go faster.

Ed was in the 15 & 16-year old age group, while Artie was in the 17 & 18-year old age group. Artie also saw Debbie was checking in for the 17 & 18-year old girls' 1,500-meter race and wished her good luck.

Ted told Artie that USATF had the 1,500 meters at their meets instead of the Mile or 1,600 meters because the 1,500 meters was the Olympic distance. Artie checked his copy of *The Big Gold Book,* and it said that the standard conversion was to multiply the seconds in a 1,500-meter time by 1.08 to calculate an equivalent mile time in seconds.

On a 200-meter indoor track, there were 7.5 laps in a 1,500 meter race. Debbie ran first and finished third in a field of five with a time of 4:58.05. Ed won his race in a time of 4:37.26. Artie finished second out of six runners in his age group with a time of 4:25.70.

Sean easily beat all the other walkers and even lapped several competitors. The boys and girls from both the older age groups all walked together but for separate medals. Sean was pleased with his time of 6:25.85 to start the season. He hoped to receive invitations to adult walking races during the indoor season and get on early performance lists.

The relays combined the older two age groups into one 15 to 18-year old age group. Bruce anchored the 4x200 relay team only to a fourth-place finish, but at least the team broke the 1:40 mark indoors with a time of 1:39.28.

The Strider team easily won the 4x800 relay. Sean led off in 2:03.3, Ed ran 2:07.8, Artie ran 2:06.7, and Tommy ran 1:59.1. It added up to 8:16.90 – a respectable time to start the season.

There were practices on the next two days, but none on New Year's Eve. Sue Evans had already headed back to the West Coast and Ed Glavine was away at a family gathering. Ted, however, was around several more days until going back to law school. In the early afternoon, He and Artie ran three easy miles, and then Artie ran three faster miles by himself.

Later, the Stewart's hosted their annual New Year Eve's party for local friends. The adults were upstairs, and the younger crowd, mostly Artie's teammates, was in the basement. Debbie arrived, and she and Ted talked about the upcoming year.

One of the Stewarts' family friends was Judge Jim Hanley. He had been a judge at the County Courthouse for over a decade. In his younger days, had been a high jumper for Coach Mallory and knew Uncle Jack quite well.

Upon Judge Hanley's arrival, he immediately went over to Ted near the Christmas tree in the living room and wanted to know all about Ted's first semester in law school. He knew a couple of Ted's law professors and enjoyed Ted's stories about the law school classes.

After a few minutes, Judge Hanley glanced under the Christmas tree and saw the monogrammed attaché case that Ted had received.

"That is a beautiful gift, Ted," said Judge Hanley. "TIS the season to be jolly! I know what the 'T' and the 'S' stand for in the monogram, but what about the 'I' in the middle?"

"It stands for Isaiah," answered Ted.

"Is that the name of a relative?"

"No, it is the name of a Professor at the Wharton School. When my dad started out as a teaching assistant, and Mom was a graduate student getting her master's degree in accounting, Professor Fisher and his wife Esther played matchmakers. My middle name is Isaiah and Margaret's middle name is Esther. I met the Professor and his wife at the Philly Relays a few years ago."

"That is an interesting story, Ted. I always wondered how your parents met."

Judge Hanley and Ted continued talking. Meanwhile, in the basement, various friends of Artie had assembled – mostly from the boys' and girls' teams. There was a big screen on one wall which was showing a New Year's Eve show with the sound turned down. There was music in the background. Some of his friends were gaming, and some were discussing New Year's resolutions – which included their track & field goals for the coming winter and spring.

Mr. & Mrs. Stewart came down to the basement periodically to refresh the refreshments. As the clock approached midnight, all eyes turned to the New Year's Eve show on the screen with the volume now turned up. Everyone watched as the ball began to drop at Times Square. The countdown commenced.

"Ten, nine, eight, seven, six, five, four, three, two, one - Happy New Year!"

Everyone raised their glasses of soda or juice and toasted the New Year by singing Auld Lang Syne.

It promised to be an interesting year.

CHAPTER TWENTY-TWO: EARLY JANUARY

On January 2nd, Artie returned to school. Practices resumed with Mr. Wimble. Ted came to the first couple of practices. He introduced himself to the coach, helped time the workouts, told him about the USATF development meet, and offered suggestions. Mr. Wimble invited Ted to come to any practices or meets whenever he was home from the law school.

Green Ridge High School had promised senior class monthly outings in their last semester. The PTA had helped raise funds to subsidize the outings. During the first week of classes in the new year, there was an announcement that the January outing would be a trip to see a matinee of the musical *Camelot*.

Arthur's English Class discussed the musical. The teacher noted that *Camelot* is fictional, but that Historians believe there was a real Arthur that led to the legendary figure. He asked if anyone knew anything about the real Arthur. Artie's grandfather and namesake had told Artie all about King Arthur. Artie raised his hand and spoke:

"Some historians believe that Arthur lived in the late fifth century during the Dark Ages after the fall of the Roman Empire. The Roman soldiers had withdrawn from England and Anglo-Saxons had invaded and occupied the east coast of England. They threatened to conquer the rest of the British Isles."

"A very grim picture," responded the teacher. "And where does Arthur fit in?"

Another Long Run

Artie continued: "Arthur may have been a Briton and a great military figure that may have stopped the Anglo-Saxons in a series of battles and brought peace to England for a generation. After he died, the Anglo-Saxons resumed their assault and conquered the rest of England. Britons fled to Wales and Scotland."

"Very good, Artie," said the teacher.

Bear Dundy, the center on the football team, raised his hand and said in a loud voice:

"I do not get it. The guy ended up being on the losing side. He is just a loser to me."

The teacher responded: "Historical figures eventually die. What is important is what each person does while alive. Keep in mind that the Anglo-Saxon kings that followed Arthur for centuries are nearly forgotten in history until Alfred the Great comes along several hundred years later. And keep in mind that the Anglo-Saxons eventually lost to the Normans in 1066. Meanwhile, King Arthur became an inspiration and an important figure in British literature in the middle-ages and his legend lives on today as we shall see next week. Overall, Arthur had a good long run."

The teacher gave Artie a wink and the class continued. Artie was looking forward to seeing the musical the following week.

After school, the team had another practice. January was a difficult month. When the weather was icy, they could not practice on the school's outdoor track and had to try to practice in the hallways or the gym. And the day of the senior outing to the musical, they got back to school too late to practice.

Artie did have one fallback option: his dad had an indoor treadmill. When there was severe weather, he could use it to do miles inside while listening to music or watching something on the wide screen in the family room wall. He even invited Sean, Tommy, and Ed to use it during or after a snowstorm.

A couple of weeks went by quickly. The senior class did attend *Camelot* and Artie liked it very much. It was easy to identify with a leading character named Arthur. Artie did not think that the real Arthur ever pulled a sword out of a stone, or that if there was a real Merlin, that he could not perform any magic tricks. His grandfather also told him that around the year 500 AD, leaders lived in wooden structures, not stone castles, nor were knights dressed in shining armor and there were no historical records of round tables. A thousand years later, authors of the Arthurian legend assumed that Arthur lived in the same circumstances that existed in the Middle Ages when, in fact, he lived in antiquity.

One thing that impressed Artie very much was the production of the musical itself. The actors and the sets were outstanding. Previously, he had only seen high school plays which were fine, but this was at another whole level. He hoped that future outings for the senior class would be as enjoyable.

CHAPTER TWENTY-THREE: MID JANUARY

Buddy McGurk had placed only two indoor track & field meets on the January schedule: the NEIL development meet, which was two weeks after school started, and the County Relays two weeks later. Both meets were at the Meadow County Community College Fieldhouse. The fieldhouse was the site for college basketball on Saturdays and Sundays, but the County High School Track Coaches Association had an agreement with the college to use it from 4 PM to 10 PM every Friday in January and February. Even on weekends when varsity athletes were busy elsewhere, there were Friday track & field meets for the frosh students at the fieldhouse.

Artie was surprised that McGurk even let them go to the development meet, but Mr. Wimble told him that there were no entry fees. Instead, each NEIL school paid one-eighth of the cost of the meet. Since Green Ridge was paying for it anyway, McGurk figured they might as well make use of the meet.

The fieldhouse was a serviceable facility. The track was 200-meters around the oval and flat with a rubber-type surface. However, it only had four lanes all the way around. There were six lanes on the home stretch for the 55-meter Dash and Hurdles.

The Fieldhouse had a sand pit for the Long Jump and Triple Jump. However, the runway for those jumps was the outside lane of the track on the back straight.

Therefore, during much of the first part of the meet, the schedule called for the 55-meter hurdles and 55-meter dash trials and finals to be held on the home stretch, while the long jump was held on the back stretch. To make it all fit within the time schedule, unlike in the other events, each school could only have three boys and three girls in the long jump and each jumper could only do four attempts.

Bruce Griffin entered the hurdle event, and both the long jump and high jump. He scooted back and forth between the two sides of the track to run his races and make his attempts in the long jump. The jump officials, aware of his situation, cooperated and let him jump out of the regular order when necessary. After the hurdles and long jump, he went over to the high jump. Bruce won a gold, silver, and bronze medal for his efforts. No one else from Green Ridge placed in the hurdles, dash, or jumps.

When the oval events finally started on the track, they began with the 400 meters in which the runners ran in lanes for the two turns of the first lap in the two-lap event. Thus, there were only four runners per section and lots of sections. Green Ridge had only Michael Thomas and sophomores who did not place.

In the 800 meters, Tommy was in the top-seeded section and did not disappoint. He broke 2 minutes with a time of 1:58.81 for an easy victory. Sean followed up with a third-place finish in the Mile in a time of 4:36.42 behind Chris Spiers and a Riverside runner.

The 3,000-meter run remained before the relays, and both Artie and Ed entered it. The race was fifteen laps long and all twenty of the boys were in a single section. The rule of the meet was that any runner lapped in the first half-mile (4 laps) had to drop out.

It was a crowded race over the first couple laps before the runners began to space out. Two runners lapped in the early going had to leave the track, reducing the field to eighteen. Artie hit the mile mark (a bit over eight laps) with a split of 4:52 and Ed at 4:59 in seventh and ninth place, respectively. Gradually, Artie narrowed the gap on the runner immediately ahead of him and on the eleventh lap, he moved into sixth place. Just before he heard the bell up ahead, he moved up another place and held on during the final lap, finishing fifth in a time of 9:06.25. That was okay for the early season. Ed finished eighth in 9:18.03.

The USATF meet had a race walk between the individual running events and the relays – giving Artie and Ed some extra recovery time. However, in the development meet, the relays immediately followed the 3,000 meters. Each of the eight schools entered a team in each relay event. Since the 4x200 and 4x400 relays start in lanes, they each had two boys' sections and two girls' sections.

Bruce Griffin anchored behind three sophs to win the slower section of the 4x200.

Next up was the 4x800 which was the penultimate event of the evening. Thankfully, the girls ran the relay first, giving Artie and Ed some extra minutes of recovery time.

After the girls, the boys lined up for the 4x800 relay. All eight teams were in one section. Sean led off and handed off the baton in second place behind Riverside. Ed and Artie ran the middle legs. They were both hurting from the short recovery time but doggedly hung close to Riverside. Tommy anchored and on the last lap showed his excellent kick, flying by the Riverside runner on the back stretch to a solid victory in 8:16.80.

Afterwards, the boys learned that they had all run within a fraction of a second of their relay splits at the USATF meet. Sean and Tommy were a fraction of a second faster, while Ed and Artie were fractions slower. Given the lack of recovery time after the 3,000-meter race, Artie was pleased with the time – and the medal.

Michael anchored the Green Ridge team to finish second in the slower section of the 4x400. The meet ended and the Green Ridge athletes had times and marks on the season's performance lists to help them in the seeding for future meets.

CHAPTER TWENTY-FOUR: LATE JANUARY

The Green Ridge team now had two weeks to gear up for their first big indoor meet of the Season – the County Relays back at the fieldhouse. The meet included six relay events on the track (shuttle hurdles, 4x200, 4 x400, 4x800, and the two medleys). There were also three field event relays (high jump, long jump, and shot put). A team in a field event relay had three athletes compete and their best marks added together for a combined mark.

Artie knew that beating Riverside looked insurmountable this year, but he wanted Green Ridge to make as strong a showing as possible. For that to happen, Green Ridge hoped to score in eight of the nine events. Scoring was 10 +8 + 6 + 4 + 2 + 1 for the top six places. In other words, there were 31 points in each of nine events which equaled 279 points up for grabs. A perfect score was 90 points – winning all nine events. The winning team usually had at least 60 points.

Bruce Griffin was the only athlete on the team who would quadruple: the hurdles, two jumps, and the 4x200 meters. Artie, Sean, Ed, Michael, and a couple soph sprinters would double.

The big question mark involved Tommy. The issue was what do about the sprint medley and 4x800 meters later in the meet. They were back-to-back events with only a girls 4x800 section in between. Normally, a half-miler would not attempt to do both events with so little recovery time. But Green Ridge needed Tommy in both events. Tommy said he could do it.

In the early events, Bruce was on four scoring relays teams. The Green Ridge shuttle hurdle team and long jump team both finished third, the 4x200 team was sixth, and the high jump team also third place thanks to his 6'0" jump. That totaled 19 points. The distance medley of Artie (1,200 meters), Michael (400 meters), Ed (800 meters), and Sean (1600 meters) finished second, and Chuck led the shot put team to a fifth place finish.

Altogether, Green Ridge had a respectable 29 points with three events remaining: the Sprint Medley, 4x800, and 4x400 relay. They did not expect to score in the 4x400 with a junior and three sophomores in it.

In the Sprint Medley, Green Ridge was in the top seeded section of four teams. Michael Thomas led off on the 400 meter leg in third place. The Carter cousins ran nice 200 meter legs and moved Green Ridge into second place behind Riverside. Tommy got the baton for the 800 meter anchor leg and just hung behind the Riverside anchor runner for three and a half laps. The pace was slow which suited him fine. Coming off the last turn, he went wide and passed the leader with about thirty meters to go and hit the finish line in first place by about a meter.

Tommy was winded but walked around while the girls ran their 4x800. Mr. Wimble came over and told him he had gone out in 61.5 for the first 400 meters and kicked faster with a 59.3 for the second 400. Coaches call this Negative Splits – the sign of a strong runner!

Shortly thereafter, the boys lined up for their 4x800 meter relay.

Sean led off and kicked on the last lap to give Green Ridge an early lead. The second leg for Riverside immediately went past Ed, but Ed hung with the Riverside runner the rest of the way. The third leg for Riverside went out fast and created a gap between him and Artie, But the leader paid a price for the pace and on the last lap, Artie narrowed the gap and nearly caught him back. Artie passed the baton to Tommy only a couple steps behind.

Tommy was running against a different anchor leg for Riverside this time, but his strategy was much the same. He hung close behind the leader for three laps conserving his remaining energy. This time, he kicked a bit earlier – on the back stretch of the bell lap – and had the lead by the final turn. He won by about two meters. Afterwards, the boys got their splits: 2:00.7 for Sean, 2:06.4 for Ed, 2:05.2 for Artie, and 2:00.5 for Tommy. It added up to 8:12.8. That would move them higher on the performance lists!

Green Ridge did not score in the 4x400 and finished with 49 points, behind Riverside (65 points), and Meadow Regional (54 points). They beat Fairmont (43 points) which was the top scoring Class 4A team in the County. The captains would get the results to Mrs. Mallory to post on social media for the alumni. The team had certainly exceeded expectations.

CHAPTER TWENTY-FIVE: EARLY FEBRUARY

Artie, Bruce, and Chuck felt the team was in full gear and ready to go into the big part of the indoor schedule.

February was championship month in the indoor track & field season: a total of five championship meets in four weeks. The NEIL and District Championships were on the first two weekends. Then the County Championships were on President's Day. And the State Classified Championships and All-Star Championships on the final two weekends of the month. A packed schedule to be sure!

First was the league meet in the fieldhouse on the first Friday of February. This was a different meet.

The district meet on the following weekend would have twelve standard indoor events: six individual track events (55 meter hurdles, 55 meter dash, 400 meters, 800 meters, Mile, and 3,000 meters), 3 field events (High Jump, Long Jump, and Shot Put), and three relays (4x200, 4x400, and 4x800 meters).

However, the league and county meets added five less common indoor track events (300, 500, 600, 1,000, and 1,500-meters). And this year, they had added an extra field event: the Pole Vault. The State All-Star Meet was adding the Pole Vault but instead of qualifying through the District & State Classified Meets, they were simply taking the top vaulters on the state performance list. The local coaches added the event to their meets wanting to give the pole-vaulters extra opportunities to improve their season's best marks.

In all, the league and county meets each had eighteen events. With 31 points awarded in each event (= 10 + 8 + 6 + 4 + 2 +1), that meant there were 558 points available for scoring in each meet. In the NEIL meet, eight schools would split the points. Each school could enter up to three athletes in each individual event, and one team in each relay event. But each athlete could only compete in one individual track event, one field event, and one relay event.

The prior meets on the schedule had not held some events early in the season, making it difficult to seed those events, but NEIL had a retired coach who conducted a seeding meeting of the coaches online early in the week of the league meet. They finalized the entries along with the sections, heats, and lane assignments for each track athlete and relay team.

In the Shot Put and Long Jump, the coaches agreed that any third-best athletes from each team should go first in random order, followed by the second-best athletes from each team in random order, followed by the best athletes from each team in random order. Of course, no team other than Riverside had three entries in both events.

Riverside was the heavy favorite to win the NEIL meet. Usually, the winning team ended up with as many as a quarter of the total points.

Green Ridge did not have enough athletes to match Riverside. They only had one or two athletes entered per event who were likely to score. Still, the team wanted to finish as high in the point standings as possible. Finishing in the top three teams in in the meet certainly was possible.

The order of the track events was also a bit unusual but took into consideration that athletes were not doubling in two individual track events.

The track schedule looked like this:

1. 55 meter hurdles (trials and finals)
2. 55 meter dash (trials and finals)
3. 3,000 meter run

4. Mile run
5. 1,000 meter run
6. 800 meter run
7. 1,500 meter run
8. 500 meter run
9. 300 meter run
10. 600 meter run
11. 400 meter run
12. 4x200 meter relay
13. 4x800 meter relay
14. 4x400 meter relay.

Another reason for the order was simple. Championship long jumps took extra time. All the jumpers would take three "trial" attempts. However, the top eight girls and top eight boys each also would take three more "final" attempts for a total of six jumps. And they needed the outside lane on the back straight as a runway for all of it. Cones were set up to keep it off limits to the runners while the long jumps were in progress.

Fortunately, the hurdles and dashes were on the other side of the track, and the distance events did not need the outside lane on the back stretch. By the time that the events run in lanes on the oval were held, the long jump would be over.

Artie was pleased with the order of events. It would give the 4x800 relay team plenty of time to recover after their individual events. He was to run in the 3,000-meters and Tommy in the 800-meter. A big question had been whether Sean should run the Mile or the 1,500 meters. They knew that Chris Spiers and the top Riverside miler were going to run the Mile, so Sean chose the 1,500 meters, and Ed entered the 1,000 meters.

The other question was which event should Michael Thomas enter? The 300, 400, 500, or 600 meters were all options. The 500 meters looked to have the weakest opposition, and Michael chose it as his event.

Green Ridge got off to a good start as Bruce Griffin won his trial heat in the hurdles and came back to win the finals in a minor upset. Green Ridge had no one qualify for the dash finals. Artie was up next in the 3,000 meters. He was in better racing shape than he had been in the development meet. He sat in 4th place for most of the fifteen laps but made a push with three laps to go to pass a tired Overlook runner and win third place and a bronze medal in a time of 8:56.50.

Green Ridge was shutout in the Mile, but Ed took fifth in the 1,000 meters (2:38.22), and Tommy outkicked the field in the 800 meters in a winning time of 1:58.01. Sean made it back-to-back victories by winning the 1,500 meters in a time of 4:09.37. Word reached them from the field events that Chuck had finished fifth in the shot put (53'2.5") and with Bruce only allowed in one field event, no Green Ridge athletes scored in the long jump.

Nine events were complete, and the meet was half over. Green Ridge had 40 points. Riverside was way ahead, Meadow Regional was a solid second, and Green Ridge in a tight battle for third place with Overlook and Spring Valley.

In the next four events on the track, only Michael Thomas broke through to score for Green Ridge. The 500 meters ran in lanes during the first two turns of the 2.5 lap event. There were a dozen runners divided into three sections, each with four runners to allow that every runner have a separate lane at the start. Michael was in the middle section and broke to the inside after the second turn in first place and held it the rest of the way to finish in a time of 1:13.33. His time did not beat anyone in the fastest section but topped everyone in the slowest section, earning him fifth place overall and two points.

Moments later, Bruce cleared 6 feet on his first attempt at that height to win the High Jump on a tiebreaker. One other jumper also cleared 6 feet but only on his second attempt after a miss. Green Ridge did not have anyone score in the Pole Vault. Only the three relay events left, Green Ridge had 52 points - two points ahead of Spring Valley and two points behind Overlook for third place.

The 4x200 meter relay split into two sections of four teams each. Because of their performance in the NEIL Development meet, Green Ridge was in the fast section. Green Ridge sophomores would run the first three legs and Bruce Griffin would run anchor leg.

The first leg of the relay ran entirely in lanes and the Green Ridge soph was in last place but close handing off the baton to the second leg who broke to the inside lane. Green Ridge stayed in last place during the second and third legs and the baton was handed off to Bruce.

As soon as Bruce Griffin got the baton, he began making up ground on the Overlook runner ahead of him. He swung wide coming out of the last turn and the two runners were dead even in the final meters. Bruce did a perfect lean as Coach Mallory had taught him – after all it is the torso that counts at the finish line – and edged out his opponent by inches.

Green Ridge and Overlook both beat all the times of the slower-seeded heat of the 4x200 relay and finished in third and fourth place overall in the event. The two teams were deadlocked in the point standings. Spring Valley did not score and trailed both teams by eight points.

The 4x800 meter relay was next up and Green Ridge did not disappoint. They led from start to finish and with the extra recovery time, all four runners improved their splits from two weeks prior: Sean (2:00.2), Ed (2:06.5), Artie (2:05.2), and Tommy (1:57.5). The relay team broke 8:10 for the first time with an 8:09.41 clocking which would move Green Ridge up the performance lists very nicely.

The relay victory also moved Green Ridge nine points ahead of Overlook and ten points ahead of Spring Valley despite a tremendous kick by Chris Spiers to move up from fifth to second on the 4x800 anchor leg.

The 4x400 meter relay concluded the meet. Overlook was the favorite to win the event, but all Green Ridge had to do was score two points to beat Overlook in the team scores. Green Ridge had a team of three juniors and Michael Thomas. If they won the slower-seeded section, they would clinch at least fifth place even if they were slower than all four teams in the faster-seeded section.

The Green Ridge lead-off leg handed off in second place, but the second leg took a small lead which the third leg kept. Michael took the baton on the anchor leg ahead by about two meters. On the second lap, a Spring Valley runner tried to pass him twice but to no avail. The miles that Michael had run in cross-country gave him some extra strength and he held off his opponent right to the end. Green Ridge also broke 3:40 with a time of 3:38.68.

The final team score was Riverside 146, Meadow Regional 104, Green Ridge 70, Overlook 69, Spring Valley 59, and the remaining 110 points divided among the other three schools. Bruce Griffin, with two gold medals and a bronze medal, was the MVP of the meet.

CHAPTER TWENTY-SIX: MID FEBRUARY

Artie figured Saint Valentine's Day was as good a time as any to ask Debbie if she would go with him to the Senior Prom in June. Deposits were due soon. As much as he was still a little reluctant to make commitments yet, Debbie was growing on him, and she was a runner. He really did think he ought to go to the prom and certainly did not want to attend stag. He had also noticed the prom pictures of Ted and Sue in the house. He knew that the prom was important.

Debbie hesitated a bit when Artie asked. She did not want to seem too eager. But she did say yes and that was that. She also made Artie agree that he would not wear sneakers to the event.

The next indoor track & field meet was the North District Qualifier. It was a difficult qualifying meet. In cross-country and spring track & field, the state had four districts, but there were fewer teams in indoor track & field, and the state had only two indoor districts: a North meet at the Liberty City Armory, and a South meet at the Red Brook Fieldhouse.

There were only eight qualifiers in each event in each class: the top three places in each event at each of the two districts plus two wild cards would advance to the State Classified Championships which was the following weekend at the State University.

The math was simple at the district meet. Sixth place scored a point. Fourth or fifth place scored more points and the chance at being a wild card qualifier to the State Meet. Second or third place scored still more points and earned a medal and automatic qualifier to the State

Meet. First place earned the most points, a medal, a qualifier, and the title of North or South Champion.

The time schedule for the district meet divided the weekend among the four classifications. The small schools in Class A competed on Friday after school. Class 2A and 3A split the schedule on Saturday. The large schools in Class 4A finished on Sunday afternoon.

As well as things had gone at the league meet, things did not seem to go well at the district meet for Green Ridge.

First, Bruce Griffin got out leaned in the hurdle finals to finish second. None of the Green Ridge Knights even made it to the final in the dash. In the Mile, Sean got outkicked and finished fourth. He would have to wait to see if he got a wild card into the State Meet. Michael Taylor won the fourth seeded section of the 400 meters but did not break into the overall scoring of the event.

Finally, Tommy O'Leary won the 800 meters, improving his best time for the season to 1:57.40. And word came from the field events that Chuck had finished 4th in the shot put (53'10"), and Bruce had added a third place in the high jump (6'0"), and a fourth place in the long jump (20'2").

Artie was next up in the 3,000 meters. There were two sections and Artie was in the faster-seeded section. Although the faster section more often goes last, the games committee decided to have it go first in this instance to allow more recovery time for better runners doubling back in the relays.

It was a crowded start to the race with some elbowing and a few close calls, but nobody fell. Eventually there was a front pack of four runners, then a gap, then a secondary pack of five, and then the rest. Artie was in the middle of the secondary pack, his group hit 4:51 for the mile.

An Overlook runner and Artie really worked the next five laps of the race and two in their pack dropped back. Over the final 400 meters, the Overlook runner, Artie, and a Huntington County runner vied for fifth place. Artie ended up splitting the two opponents to finish in sixth with 8:56.33 for a time. It was not a qualifier to the State meet, but at least it earned a point for the team. Ed Glavine won the slower-seeded section of the event breaking nine minutes with a time of 8:59.76.

In the 4x200 relay, Green Ridge won the second fastest section, but only bested the time of one of the six teams in the fastest seeded heat, to earn Green Ridge another single point.

The Green Ridge 4x800 relay team felt the effects of a shorter recovery time and were a bit off their performance at the league meet, but still managed to win handily with 8:10.42 as the winning time.

In the 4x400 relay, the Green Ridge team won the third section of the event but did not break into the scoring.

Overall, Green Ridge scored 48 points to place fifth in the team scoring. Bruce, Tommy, and the 4x800 relay team had qualified for the State Classified Championships. Sean and Chuck were also wild card possibilities.

CHAPTER TWENTY-SEVEN: LATE FEBRUARY

Green Ridge scheduled another outing for the Senior Class in February on the Friday before Presidents Day. The class went to a National Park that had George Washington's winter headquarters during two winters of the Revolutionary War and the nearby site of the winter encampment of his soldiers.

First, the school buses took the senior class to the mansion in the park that was Washington's winter headquarters. There were hourly guided tours by Park Rangers.

Artie could not help but think that while it may have been considered a nice mansion at the time, it did not have modern conveniences such as a refrigerator, a modern stove, and running water in the kitchen. Also, no indoor bathrooms, no electricity, and most of all, no central heating. The fireplaces and blankets were all that was available to keep warm at night.

Still, to be sure, it was amazing to think that George Washington, Alexander Hamilton, and other Founding Fathers lived almost 250 years ago where Artie was standing.

After the tour, the class went to a visitor center and gift shop for a while. After that, they boarded the bus to go to a different area a few miles away in the location where the soldiers' encampment had been. The area was known as the "Hollow." It was near woods and the soldiers had cut down trees to build makeshift huts. The school bus took the students to another Visitor Center at which there was a replica hut that the visitors could view up close.

The school had provided the students with box lunches which they ate in the school bus or tailgating. It was too cold to picnic on the grounds.

Afterwards, the students went inside the Visitor Center at the Hollow and saw a video presentation of an actor playing a soldier struggling through the awful winter that took place in 1779-1780. Many of the casualties during the war were not on the battlefield but instead soldiers that did not survive the winters or succumbed to diseases for which there were no known cures at the time. It all made Artie appreciate the sacrifices made to allow the United States to become a free country.

There were well-marked trails at the Hollow. The longest was more than six miles long, but the students did not have enough time to walk it. Instead, they chose the shorter "Yellow Trail" which was only two+ miles long. Even in winter, it was very scenic. The students took pictures of the well-kept grounds with their smartphones. Artie was glad that this was one of the senior class outings.

It occurred to Artie that it would be possible to create a great cross country course on the site. However, he realized it would not be in keeping with its historical nature. Soldiers had suffered and even died there. There should be respect for the site.

The school buses returned to school in time to do light jogging to loosen up for the big weekend meets. Practices during the week had been short and fast as it was time to peak and rest before the major meets: the State Classified Championships on Saturday and the County Championships on Presidents Day.

On the same Friday after the school outing, Artie went to watch the Frosh County Championships at the fieldhouse.

On Saturday, six athletes from Green Ridge headed down to the State Classified Championships: Bruce Griffin, Tommy O'Leary, Chuck James, and the 4x800 relay team including Tommy on the anchor leg.

The State meet was at the State Athletic Center (SAC) at State University. The SAC was huge - much larger than a simple community college fieldhouse or Liberty State Armory at which the boys had competed previously. The SAC had a banked 200-meter track with six lanes on the oval and eight lanes on the straight. And there was plenty of space to have excellent field event venues as well.

With only eight qualifiers per event in each classification, every event was a final and the meet was in a single day. The small schools (Class A and Class 2A) started together in the morning, and the large schools (Class 3A and 4A) followed together in the afternoon and evening.

With every event a final and more lanes available, the meet moved along efficiently. Only the 400-meters and 4x200 and 4x400 relay split into two sections.

Bruce took a couple of third places in the hurdles and high jump plus a fifth in the long jump. Chuck managed to top 54 feet for the first time (by a whole half inch!) and beat two of the eight shot putters to earn a point. Tommy unleashed a furious kick to pass two opponents on the final straight to become the Class 3A Champion in the 800 meters. His time of 1:56.88 was a personal best.

The final event for Green Ridge was the 4x800 relay and the relay team wanted to keep their unbeaten streak alive.

Sean led off and was in third place after the first lap. He bided his time and on his last lap made a move on the back straight of his final lap to move ahead of the runner in front of him to hand off the baton to Ed in second place behind the Riverside runner. Ed was under orders to try to hang behind Riverside until trying to kick on the last lap.

After Ed completed his third lap, Artie went to the exchange zone and awaited the baton handoff. He could see Ed was tiring and coming off the last turn, a runner from the South district went wide and passed him. Artie started waving at Ed and yelled: "Bring it in, bring it in!" 40 meters, 30 meters, 20 meters and only ten meters to go. Ed outstretched his arm holding the baton and placed it in Artie's hand. Artie was off and running in third place.

Artie did not know much about the runner ahead of him from the South district. But the pace was good, so he tucked in behind him for the first two laps. He thought about what to do next. The other runner was expecting a challenge to come on the last lap. However, Artie did not want the third leg to come down to a kick and thought he might catch his opponent by surprise by doing something else.

Artie remembered that Ted had once told him that often the third 200 meters was the key to an 800-meter race. So, he began his lift early – at the beginning of the home stretch before their final lap and went right by the South runner. He still had to hold on to second place the whole last lap and that he did. Now it was up to Tommy.

Tommy took the baton about eight meters behind the same Riverside runner he had beaten earlier in the individual 800 meter event. He did not try to make up the entire deficit right away. Whittling it down bit by bit was the better way to do it. With three laps to go, he was six meters back. With two laps to go, he was four meters back. At the bell, he was only about two meters behind.

Coming off the penultimate turn, Tommy went wide into the backstretch and tried to pass the Riverside runner, but his opponent held him off. He tried again near the end of the straight but had no more success. He regrouped yet again and went wide coming off the last turn. The two runners were dead even with fifty meters to go. Tommy had more strength and edged ahead to win by a half second.

As they collected their gold medals, the boys found out their splits (except for Tommy) were personal bests: Sean (2:00.4), Ed (2:05.7), Artie (2:05.0), and Tommy (1:57.3) totaling 8:08.43 - their best time of the year. Green Ridge ended the day with 35 points, which was good enough for seventh place in the Class 3A team standings.

On Sunday, Artie studied for his physics and Spanish exams.

On Presidents Day, The County meet was much like the league meet except more schools – teams from the NIL, NSL, and even from the Tri-County Conference as well as the NEIL. There were the same eighteen events and the same 558 points available. As was with the

NEIL meet, each athlete could only compete in one individual track event, one field event, and one relay.

To make the County meet work in the limited time available and more schools than in the league meet, entry into the County meet was more difficult. In the NEIL meet, each team could enter up to three athletes per event. In the County meet, a team could only enter one athlete per event unless it had one or two additional athletes that exceeded standards showing the additional athletes had a serious chance to score.

The stringent qualifying did not affect Green Ridge very much since it had a squad only big enough to enter a single athlete that was a scoring threat in most events. Their athletes usually entered the same events as they had at the NEIL meet, giving them a suitable time or mark for a seed. This would be the final indoor meet of the indoor season for much of the squad.

Bruce Griffin started the competition with another victory in the hurdles - as close as at the NEIL meet. Again, however, the Knights did not score in the dash.

The 3,000 meter run was next. Artie stayed in a lead pack of no less than seven runners during the first ten laps. Then things got interesting. There were surges to break things up. Three runners broke away with 600 meters to go. Artie shook off two of the others in the last laps but was outkicked by the other runner to finish fifth (8:53.33) and score two points.

Green Ridge was shutout in the Mile (which Chris Spiers won easily) but Ed scored a point in the 1,000 meters (2:37.5), and Tommy won the 800 meters, kicking after a slow pace to finish in 1:58.51 on the clock. Green Ridge did not score in the 600 meters.

In the 1,500 meters, Sean led during most of the later stages of the race but got outkicked by a Fairmont runner on the final lap to finish second in 4:08.76. Green Ridge did not score in the 500 or 300 meters. Word came back from the field events that Bruce had finished second in the high jump (6'0") and Chuck was sixth in the shot put with a throw of 53'10" but Green Ridge did not score in the Long Jump or Pole Vault.

Add it all up and Green Ridge had 40 points with the three relays left in the meet.

In the 4x200 relay, Bruce anchored Green Ridge to win the second section, but Green Ridge did not beat the times of any of the teams in the fast section and took fifth overall.

Green Ridge notched another victory in the 4x800 relay. The pace was a little off, but Sean, Ed and Artie gave Tommy a lead that he did not relinquish with an 8:10.80 winning time.

The meet finished with the 4x400 relay. Even though Michael Thomas anchored Green Ridge to a win in the third section, they did not break into the top six teams overall.

In the final team point standings, Green Ridge took fifth place with 52 points behind Riverside, Meadow Regional, Fairmont, and Overlook.

On The following Saturday, the same six members of the Green Ridge team returned to the SAC for the State All-Star Meet. There was no team scoring in the meet – only the chance to claim the top spots in the state in each event. Bruce claimed fifth in the hurdles, and sixth in the High Jump and Long Jump to be one of only two athletes to score in three events. Chuck did not place despite a personal best of 54'6" on his last throw. Tommy was third in the 800 meters, lowering his indoor personal best to 1:56.32

The 4x800 relay was Green Ridge's last event of the day again. It was close but Green Ridge kept its unbeaten streak alive as Tommy edged the anchor leg of the Class 4A Championship team. And Green Ridge knocked off another two seconds off their best time. Not a bad way to end the indoor season.

CHAPTER TWENTY-EIGHT: EARLY MARCH

March was an unpredictable month in many ways. The weather could be beautiful, or it could be full of snow. The temperature could swing forty or more degrees in 24 hours. But one thing was very predictable for the Green Ridge team: lots of training.

The indoor track & field season was over – at least for the Knights. There was no way that Buddy McGurk was interested in sending anybody to the Eastern Championships or one of the National meets.

The three track & field captains reviewed their checklist for the start of the spring season:

T was for Training. Ted and other alumni who had been giving suggested workouts for the indoor season would continue for the spring. The team also needed workouts for the additional outdoor events.

R was for Recruitment. There were a few athletes who had competed in other sports in the winter who were potential additions to the track & field team in the spring. The captains discussed who to approach.

A was whether to continue Avoiding Buddy McGurk. That had worked mostly okay during the indoor season.

C was for communication. The captains had already given Mrs. Mallory a preview of the spring season to put on the social media page. The support the team was getting from the alumni was proving invaluable.

K was for Kilometers. It was time to build the mileage base again before the new season started.

March was about training, training, and more training. No track & field meets (except for one scrimmage) before April. And time for team members to get ready for outdoor events. Chuck would finally get to throw his specialty, the Javelin, and try to develop some consistency in the discus as well. Bruce would add the triple jump to his repertoire. Meanwhile, Artie would try to add some double workouts into his schedule by running a few miles between home and school in the mornings.

However, there was one member of the team that was not yet ready to give up on the indoor season. Sean Allen wanted to enter the race walk in one of the national indoor meets. Although not a standard high school event, the race walk was an event in the national meets and Sean could work around McGurk.

It was simple. The national meets had expert walk coordinators to decide which entries to accept. Sean had won the race walk at the USATF National Junior Olympics last summer as a Strider. A call by his Strider race walk coach to a coordinator would get him into a national meet easy. He also hoped to do an outdoor racewalk at the adult level later in the month – to prepare him for the race walk at the Philly Relays in late April.

Ah yes, the Philly Relays at the end of April. Artie had gone as a spectator to see Ted run in it on multiple occasions. It was a great meet, and the goal of the top Green Ridge athletes was to be on the traveling team for an overnight stay in Philadelphia. Competing at the Philly Relays was the highlight of many a high school athlete's athletic career. But the deadline to enter was in late March.

Philly Relays allowed any high school to enter the 4x100 relay and qualifying for the 4x400 relay was not difficult: the Green Ridge boys had already bested the 3:40 qualifying time twice during the indoor season. The 4x800 relay had a tougher qualifying standard but the boys' time of 8:06.10 at the State All-Star meet would get them in.

Chuck had thrown the Javelin at Philly last year and the meet would accept him again. Also, the girls' 4x100 and 4x400 relay teams were eligible as well.

Artie talked to Debbie, and she was worried about the entry of the girls' relay teams too. What to do? Artie knew that talking to McGurk would be fruitless. He would delay and run out the clock until it was too late to enter. But avoidance of McGurk would not solve the problem.

On Friday evening, Ted arrived home for his spring break during the next week. Artie poured out his frustrations to Ted who was silent but listening thoughtfully. Finally, he told Artie not to get his hopes up too high, but he would make a phone call over the weekend.

On Monday morning, Buddy McGurk was sitting in his office doing planning for next fall's football season. The phone rang and he could see that the caller was Stanley Morgan, a venture capitalist and football alum. He got on the phone immediately.

"Hello, is that you, Stan?"

"It sure is, Buddy, how has life been treating you?"

"Fine, Fine. I have been meaning to give you a call. You know we came close to that State Championship last year. A little bit more and we will be there. But we really need to renovate the exercise room and that will cost some money …"

"Let me cut you off right there. I might be receptive to helping you out with that. I have a deal to offer you."

"Great, give me the details."

'Well, you may not know that in addition to being a quarterback, I was a good javelin thrower in my time. I even held the school record until Chuck James broke it. He and the others who qualify should go down to the Philly Relays in late April – it will be a once in a lifetime experience for some of them."

"But I do not think we have anything in the budget for it, Stan."

"I figured as much, so here is the deal - I will donate to the school three thousand dollars to cover the travel and lodging expenses for the coaches and athletes to go to Philly. And once I see that they all competed in the Philly Relays, I will be receptive to underwriting the cost of renovating the exercise room. How does that sound?"

"I guess so."

"Look, Buddy. I know you are annoyed that Chuck James quit the football team, but you have only yourself to blame. He is a real talent in the Javelin. He has a chance to win in Philly and to be one of the top Javelin throwers in the country. And I know first-hand that learning to throw a forward pass and a javelin are complimentary. Both use the same basic muscle groups. You should not have given him an ultimatum to choose between the two sports."

"What is done is done."

"I know but let us not make things worse. Let Chuck and the runners have their trip, and I will see that you have your new exercise room. Deal?"

"Deal," said Buddy McGurk reluctantly.

"Good. I tell you what. The deadline for the entries for Philly Relays is near the end of this month. As soon as I get confirmation that Green Ridge has entered, I will send you the donation for the team's travel expenses and three thousand more as a deposit on the exercise room. After the Philly Relays, we will work out the rest. Now remember, the boys have three eligible relay teams, the girls have two teams, and Chuck James is in Javelin. The entry should include all of them. Got it?"

"Got it," answered Buddy McGurk as he ended the phone call. He guessed he could stomach giving the track & field squad a trip to get the renovations he wanted. He left Mr. and Mrs. Wimble a message to see him at lunchtime.

On the next day before practice, Mr. Wimble told the team that the school had added Penn Relays to the schedule in late April. There were cheers and hollering. The top members of the team now had a new goal in the first part of the spring season – to make the traveling team.

CHAPTER TWENTY-NINE: EARLY MARCH (CONTINUED)

*I*t was time for another outing: the Senior Class was off to see a music concert entitled Classical Pops. When the Senior Class arrived at the University theater, they were handed programs. The concert was meant to introduce students (most of whom had never heard live classical music) to some of the classics that had gained mainstream popularity over the years. Artie looked at the program to check what they would be hearing during the concert:

Serenade to Music by Vaughn Williams

Canon In D Major by Johann Pachelbel

The Planets by Gustav Holst

Appalachian Spring by Aaron Copeland

William Tell Overture by Gioachino Rossini

Pomp and Circumstance by Edward Elgar

Artie sat next to Debbie. He was impressed to see a whole orchestra on stage. He had been to a concert before with a rock band that only had five members.

The orchestra began to play. Artie did not know much about classical music but some of the selections sounded vaguely familiar because his dad sometimes played classics as background music while working in his home office. Artie thought he had heard *Canon in D*

Major at a cousin's wedding a couple years ago, and the William *Tell Overture* on an old television series he had watched with his grandparents. He also had heard *Pomp and Circumstance* at Ted's Graduation. The conductor said that they were doing the last number as a nod to any graduating seniors in the audience.

Artie's favorite selection was *The Planets* by Holst even though they only did the music for Mars, Venus, and Uranus. A teacher said that there was also music for each of the other planets except for Earth. He said that Holst was an English composer who wrote the music for *The Planets* in the early Twentieth Century. Some music critics believed it was the inspiration for the music of *Star Wars* and other movies.

On the bus ride home, someone got the music by Holst for the rest of the planets on their smartphone. It was excellent. Who would have thought music over a century old could sound so good?

CHAPTER THIRTY: MID MARCH

The team pushed through another week of tough practices, but Ted was home for spring break and there to help Mr. Wimble each day. Saturday was time-trial day and Ted's last day before returning to the law school. He put out a call on social media for other alumni to come help and was surprised to see a former nemesis show up and come over to shake his hand.

"Is that you, Sonny?" asked Ted.

"I go by Larry Lamar, Jr. these days," answered Lamar sheepishly.

"Well, if you are here to help the team, you're welcome," said Ted.

"I appreciate that, Ted. I know I messed up back in the day. But my brother is on the frosh team now and I want the team to do well. You are more qualified than me to teach the quarter milers, but I figure I could help with the long jump unless Kevin Bell is around to do it."

"Nope, he moved to Texas years ago. And as best I know, there are no other alumni to help the jumpers today. I do not think you have to teach Bruce Griffin much, but he is splitting his training among the hurdles and jumps and does not have much time to help the young guys. If you could work with the frosh and soph jumpers, that would be great."

"You got it."

Ted brought Larry over to introduce him to Artie who vaguely remembered him but said nothing. Then Ted and Larry went over to Bruce and Chuck to introduce them to Larry.

Most of the team alumni who were certified officials and had come to help at the December time trial were back. This would be a good warm-up for them as they would be back in three weeks to officiate at the Green Ridge Relays. Before the meet, Artie could see some of them at the finish line talking to Mr. Wimble who now had his own stopwatches and had been practicing.

The March time-trials were much like the December ones but with a few changes. This time the girls had started in the morning and just concluded. The boys followed in the early afternoon. On the track, each runner was still only doing one event, but the events had changed a bit: the hurdlers were doing the 110 meter-hurdles. Other events included the 200 meters for the sprinters, and the 400 meters and the Mile. The half-milers would run the 400 meters with the quarter-milers to see who potential candidates were to run legs in the 4x400 relay in the spring.

All the distance runners would run the mile.

The field events were no longer in the gym. It was time for the athletes to adjust to competing outdoors, even if the weather was still chilly on some days in the early season.

The time-trials went well. The weather cooperated with temperatures over sixty degrees. The trials gave the squad a chance to see where they were with their training. Other sophomores in addition to Ed Glavine seemed to show promise. And the frosh students gave hope for the future – even if they were not likely to help the varsity this year. Ted timed and watched the races closely. It would help to know the team firsthand when Artie called him during the spring with questions and to discuss the latest about the team.

Ted also talked to Mr. Wimble who said he had enjoyed this year and learned about the sport of track & field. He was under no illusions that he would have a long-term career as a track coach but hoped to fill the temporary gap satisfactorily. He wanted to stay involved in the sport after this year and had just done a clinic to get certified as a track & field official. The officials at the finish line remarked that he had come a long way in the quality of his timing.

Ted and Mr. Wimble also checked out the field events. There were new team members: a couple basketball players who could high jump, and a hockey player and a wrestler who had not been on the indoor squad were throwing with Chuck James. However, they still did not have the depth for which Coach Mallory's teams were renowned. Depth was critical for the outdoor season – especially in dual meets and the County Relays.

First up, the time-trials were a warm-up for the scrimmages next weekend.

CHAPTER THIRTY-ONE: LATE MARCH

*T*ed headed back to law school on Sunday. Meanwhile, Artie was working on a research paper about the Great Depression. He approached his dad and asked about the causes of the Great Depression – his dad was an economist after all.

Artie's dad went over to his bookcase and pulled out a slim volume *The Great Contraction* by Milton Friedman and Anna Schwartz and handed it to Artie.

"Here this will help you. It is a chapter about the Great Depression from their book *Monetary History of the United States* which is a classic."

"Thanks, dad. But what about the quote our teacher told us by a guy named Keynes that in the long run, we are all dead."

"Well Lord Keynes was a British economist whose solution in economic downturns was for the government to spend extra money to create a short-term fiscal stimulus. His critics said that in the long run, such actions cancel out, or are even detrimental. In response, Keynes made his curt remark that in the long run, we are all dead."

"Was he right?"

"Keynes was long dead by the 1970s, but his theories were so accepted that an American President supposedly said that "we are all Keynesians now." But in the 1970s, the British and American economies became a total mess with stagflation and the so-called "Misery Index" at record levels. Fortunately, both Britain and the USA rejected Keynesian economics in the 1980s and both had excellent recoveries."

"How come Keynes still gets quoted today?"

"Unfortunately, every generation needs to re-learn the lessons of history. The long run does matter eventually."

On Monday, it was back to school. Another week of difficult workouts. On Saturday, Green Ridge had its annual Spring scrimmages. The St. Joseph's boys team came to Green Ridge, while the Green Ridge girls team went to St. Mary's for their scrimmage.

The NEIL rules for dual meets did not allow for anybody to do a distance triple (Mile-800-3,000) Although some of the distance runners previously had done the triple in scrimmages to see where they stood in each event, the captains and Mr. Wimble decided to make the scrimmage more like a dress rehearsal for the dual meets and follow the NEIL rule. Artie and Ed would do a Mile/3,000 double, Sean and Tommy would do a Mile/800 double, and Tommy would also do a leg on the 4x400 relay team.

The captains reviewed the other events with Mr. Wimble. The sophomore Carter cousins (Sam and Jeff) had improved throughout the indoor season in the sprints. Bruce was clearly the best high hurdler and its top threat in all three jumps. That meant that he would need to let others on the squad do the 400 meter hurdles because of the four-event limit in the high school rule book.

In practice, Michael Thomas seemed the best on the squad in the longer hurdle event but in the order of events in the dual meets, the 400 meter hurdles directly followed the 400 meter dash. With little recovery time between the two events, Michael could only run one or the other comfortably, and then double back in the 4x400 relay which was the last event of the day. He and the others felt he had a better chance of scoring in the hurdles, and so the 400 meter dash would be for others to do in the scrimmage.

In the throws, although the javelin was Chuck's best event, he was also the Knight's biggest threat in the shot put and discus, but he lacked consistency in the latter event.

The scrimmage went well. There was no team score in a scrimmage although St. Joe's would have won by a small margin.

The boys faced their former Junior Olympic teammates - the McCauley twins and the Notto brothers. Sean edged the twins in the mile; Tommy easily won the 800 meters; and Artie and Ed finished second and third in the 3,000 meters. Bruce won three events and finished second in the triple jump. Chuck won the javelin, and the shot put and took third in the discus. The team was ready for their opening meet.

CHAPTER THIRTY-TWO: EARLY APRIL

Before the opening meet of the season, Artie got good news which diverted his attention. The State University had accepted him to be a first-year student next fall. Although he had been optimistic about his chances, it was still good getting official notification of his acceptance.

He was unsure what subject would be his major. And there was still the matter of whether he would continue running in college. His achievements as a distance runner were not of the level to get an athletic scholarship or even to be a recruit for an NCAA Division 1 team. And from what he had heard, it was difficult for a male athlete to make a team as a walk-on. But that was something to worry about later – after the spring season was over.

Meanwhile, the Senior Class was off on another field trip. This one was to an historical museum.

Artie found the museum remarkably interesting with all sorts of exhibits and videos. There were items that were hundreds of years old.

Artie particularly liked a wing of the museum dedicated to Native Americans and Indigenous People. It had photographs from the Nineteenth and Twentieth Centuries and artifacts even older. It dawned on Artie that when the Native Americans had created the artifacts hundreds of years ago, they had no idea at the time that their creations would show people today their history and culture.

Artie recognized one photograph immediately. It was a picture of Olympian Billy Mills. He had won the 10,000 meters – the longest run on the track in the Olympics – in one of the greatest upsets in track & field history at the 1964 Tokyo Olympics.

Tokyo was the last of the "older" part of the Modern Olympics. It still used a cinder track and had not yet accepted Fully Automatic Timing. And in the age before communication satellites connected Asia and North America, there was little television coverage in the USA. Films of the 1964 Summer Olympic Games went on planes from Japan to the USA just to show a few highlights on television to American audiences. Four years later, everything changed with the 1968 Mexico City Olympics in North America. For the first time Americans saw a Summer Olympics live hour after hour on television.

As a result of the above, Olympic heroes in 1968 are still much better known than Olympic heroes in 1964. Fortunately, a movie *Running Brave* was later made telling the story of Billy Mills. Artie had seen the movie. The museum showed a short clip from it.

On the day after the Museum visit, the opening meet of the season was on the schedule. Green Ridge was again the #4 seed in the NEIL as it had been in cross country. In fact, the overall seeding was close to the seeding for cross country. It looked like this:

#1 Riverside

#2 Meadow Regional

3 Overlook

#4 Green Ridge

#5 Spring Valley

#6. Eastwood

#7 Arcola

8 Undercliff

For the opening week on the schedule, Green Ridge was to serve as the host to visiting teams #2 Meadow Regional and #8 Undercliff.

But nature had other ideas. A late-season storm coated Meadow County with a wintery mix that made the track too slippery to use.

Overnight the weather moderated, and Green Ridge was willing to do the meet on Thursday, but Meadow Regional thought that was too close to their weekend meet, and the three teams agreed to reschedule the meet to early May.

The postponement of the opening NEIL meet meant that the team had no competition during the first week of the season. Riverside and Green Ridge each hosted relay meets on the first two Saturdays in April as warmups for the County Relays on the third weekend.

Because Green Ridge Relays was a fund raiser with much volunteer labor from the track & field alumni, Buddy McGurk did not cancel it as he had canceled the Polar Bear Relays in December. However, he did not enter Green Ridge in the Riverside Relays on the first April weekend, and Riverside responded by not entering the Green Ridge Relays on the following weekend, indicating that they could find better competition elsewhere. Meadow Regional followed Riverside's lead.

Instead of going to a meet, Artie and the team just had an extra practice on the first Saturday and prepared for a dual meet the next week at the sixth seed which was Eastwood - coached by Jim Kowalski who had previously been the Green Ridge assistant coach for the field events. A few years ago, he had accepted the head coaching job at his alma mater. The Eastwood team had shown steady improvement under his guidance. Green Ridge was a slight favorite going into the meet, but Artie expected a close encounter.

The scoring for a dual meet is simple: Nine points available in each of fifteen individual events - five points for first place, three for second place, and one for third place. The 4x400 relay at the end is worth five points, winner takes all. There are eight individual track events (100, 200, 400, 800, Mile, 3000, and both hurdles) and seven field events (Pole Vault, the three jumps, and three throws).

It all adds up to 140 points in sixteen events in a dual meet. Getting over 70 points means a victory – like a passing grade in school.

There were intervals of slight drizzle on Wednesday afternoon, but the coaches and officials agreed to go ahead with the meet. Trying to reschedule a second postponement in the first two weeks of the season would be difficult to do.

Things did not start well for Green Ridge. In the 110 meter hurdles, Bruce crashed on the fifth hurdle and was a DNF. Eastwood also won the 100 meters and 400 meters, 400 hurdles, and 200 meters in the early going on the track while Green Ridge won only the mile and 800 meters. In the field events, Green Ridge did better: Chuck won the javelin and shot put, and Bruce won the triple jump and high jump while Eastwood won only the pole vault. However, Coach Kowalski's expertise was apparent in the depth on his team as Eastwood got most of the second and third places in the field events.

As Artie and Ed went to the starting line for the 3,000 meters, Eastwood had a slim 56-52 lead with four events left. After the first mile, Artie picked up the pace and Ed followed. After another two laps, they had broken away from the Eastwood runners and coasted to an easy 1-2 finish.

Now, Green Ridge led with a 60-57 score. If Chuck could win the Discus, and Bruce win the Long Jump, Green Ridge would at least get a tie, and if someone on the team could gain another point in the Discus or Long Jump, they would have 71 points and clinch victory. Otherwise, it would come down to the relay in which they were clear underdogs.

Bruce jumped over 21 feet on his first attempt in the Long Jump which turned out to be all he needed. But in the Discus, all was not going well. Chuck barely fouled on his first attempt and slipped in the wet circle and fouled again on his second try. On his third attempt, he took a "safety" throw, but it only put him in third place. In the final round, he had dropped to fourth place when he took his final throw. It looked good but he could not stay in the circle, fouling yet again.

Eastwood now led 70-65 with only the relay remaining. Green Ridge needed to win the relay to salvage a tie in the meet. Tommy loosened up to run the leadoff leg. He gave the Knights a temporary lead, but the Carter cousins could not keep up and Michael Thomas had a ten-meter deficit as he took the baton. He gained only a little ground the entire lap. Eastwood won the meet 75-65 in a mild upset. Getting swept in the High Hurdles and Discus had cost Green Ridge dearly.

Jim Kowalski came over to Mr. Wimble and the Green Ridge captains. He said he had just talked to Coach Mallory and was proud of the way that the Green Ridge team was carrying on in difficult circumstances. He wished them well and would see them again on Saturday at the relay meet.

CHAPTER THIRTY-THREE: MID APRIL

*T*here was not much time to dwell on the disappointing loss to Eastwood. The Knights needed to finalize their lineup for the Green Ridge Relays on Saturday. There were nine track relays (4x100, 4x200, 4x400, 4x800, 4x1600, two medleys, and two hurdle relays). Each of these required four athletes. There were also seven field event relays requiring three athletes at each.

The above totaled 57 spots to fill. Even with Bruce taking care of four of those spots, and others doubling or tripling, the team would have to fill out the lineup with untested younger members of the team.

There were 31 points awarded to the top six places in each of the sixteen relay events (= 10 + 8 + 6 + 4 + 2 +1) totaling 496 points up for grabs. For years, Green Ridge would rack up over one hundred points. They would need something near that to win it this year. Of course, the task was easier due to the absence of Riverside and Meadow Regional.

The Knights were the clear favorites in the two medleys, the 4x800, and the High Jump and Javelin relays. That would be worth fifty points. The big question was whether they could pick up enough points in the other eleven events. They would need to score in most of them.

And Green Ridge did just that.

The meet started off well as Bruce passed the Eastwood anchor leg in the Shuttle High Hurdles to grab second place, and Xavier, Yu, Zoller and Wagner surprised everybody by placing third in an admittedly weak field in the 4x1600 relay. The Knights went on to win the two medleys and 4x800, and picked up third, fourth and fifth place in the 4x100, 4x400 Hurdles (adding their four times together), and the 4x400. Their only shutout was in the 4x200 due to a dropped baton.

In the field events, Bruce led the high jumpers to a relay victory, and the long and triple jumpers to a pair of third places. Chuck led the throwers to a victory in the Javelin relay and fourth and fifth places in the Shot Put and Discus events. Even the sophomore pole vaulters earned a point by being one of only six teams to have all three vaulters clear 8'6" – the opening height.

Green Ridges total score added up to 95 points which was twelve more than Overlook and Fairmont tied for second, and fourteen points more than Eastmont. The team had its first trophy to put in the school trophy case for the season.

The following week was busy with two more meets.

The meet on the NEIL schedule was moved from Wednesday to Tuesday because the County meet started on Thursday instead of Friday because the schools were closed on Good Friday. Green Ridge faced Spring Valley (#5) and Arcola (#7) at the latter school. Neither school was as competitive as Eastwood had been. Despite a double victory by Chris Spiers in the Mile and 3,000 meters, Green Ridge led from start to finish defeating Spring Valley 81-59, and Arcola 102-38.

The County Relays were the following weekend after the Green Ridge Relays. It had the same sixteen relay events worth 496 points. The points would be harder to earn this time around with Riverside and Meadow Regional in the mix.

Artie knew that beating Riverside at the County Relays was a long shot this year. Riverside had the depth to be a threat in every event. In the end, Green Ridge was able to win four events: the Sprint Medley, 4x800, High Jump and Javelin relays. They added two second places, two thirds, a fourth, three fifths and a sixth for a total of 79 points to finish in third place. Riverside won with 111 points, and Meadow Regional was second with 98 points.

There was one more dual meet before the Philly Relays. It was on Tuesday instead of the usual Wednesday to allow travel time to the Philly Relays, which started on Thursday. The dual meet was the toughest one of the season: Green Ridge at top-seeded Riverside. In the past, the meet was always the last dual meet of the season in early May between the two powerhouses of the NEIL. Now since Green Ridge had slipped in the seedings, it was in April instead.

Artie knew that Riverside had multiple potential scorers in every event while Green Ridge would be fortunate if one of its athletes scored in most events and hoped just to avoid a Riverside sweep in its weaker events.

Artie also knew that Riverside would hunt for every available point. They did not want to win narrowly but to make the score as lopsided as possible. They had scored a hundred points against every NEIL opponent thus far, even while resting their top athletes in meets against weaker opponents. They would try to top a hundred points against Green Ridge too. Meanwhile, even If they did not win the meet, Green Ridge wanted to keep the score as close as possible.

Riverside took the early lead. Green Ridge won the events they expected: the High Hurdles, High Jump, Long Jump, Javelin, and 800 meters. They also won the Mile in a mild upset when Sean Allen outkicked the top Riverside miler. However, they could only add six second places and four thirds to the scoring resulting in an 88-52 final score.

The loss left Green Ridge with a 2-2 record in the NEIL standings with wins against Spring Valley and Arcola, and losses to Eastwood and Riverside. In May, they would still face Overlook (#3), and make-up the postponed meet against Meadow Regional (#2) and Undercliff (#8).

CHAPTER THIRTY-FOUR: LATE APRIL

The track & field relay meet is an American contribution to the sport. There are great relay meets throughout the USA in states such as Florida, Virginia, Texas, Kansas, California, and Iowa. However, the oldest and biggest of them all is in Pennsylvania.

The Philly Relays have been around since 1895 (before the Modern Olympics began) and are truly a "Carnival." It takes place at an old brick stadium near the banks of the Schuylkill River in Philadelphia and sometimes over 100,000 people attend during the three days, Thursday, Friday, and Saturday - always ending on the last Saturday in April. Competitors include grade school youngsters, high school girls and boys, college men and women, post-collegians including Olympians, and masters up to 100 years old.

The trip to Philadelphia was the only overnight trip on the Green Ridge schedule and therefore a highlight of the season. In recent years, the Philly Relays alternated between the high school girls or boys starting the meet. This year, the girls were starting on Thursday, and the boys following on Friday.

The Green Ridge girls and boys had both entered 4x100 and 4x400 relay teams and the boys had also entered the 4x800 relay and Chuck James in the Javelin. Plus, Sean Allen was entered as a Strider in the walk which did not have a high school boys' event. The girls traveled to Philadelphia on Wednesday afternoon. The boys followed on Thursday afternoon.

Nine boys were making the trip. Sean, Ed, Artie, and Tommy were running the 4x800 relay early on Friday morning and Chuck would throw the javelin early that morning. Michael, Jeff & Sam Carter, and Bruce were running the 4x100 relay later Friday morning. On Saturday morning, Sean would compete in the 5,000-meter race walk, while Tommy, the Carter cousins, and Michael would double back to run the 4x400 relay.

The boys went down to Philadelphia in two vehicles. Coach Wimble drove an SUV with the 4x800 squad and Chuck James. The wrestling coach Darren Logan drove the 4x100 squad in a car. They figured having two vehicles would give them more flexibility than a bus.

In the past, the athletic directors often went to the Philly Relays with the team, but Artie had not seen Buddy McGurk around lately. He figured McGurk was off to spring football coaching conferences, and that McGurk would not want to attend the Philly Relays anyway. On the other hand, Mr. Logan seemed like a good guy and had done overnight trips with wrestlers attending the state championships in the southern part of the state.

Wednesday had started out sunny, but showers developed on the ride to Philadelphia. Chuck, Sean, and Tommy had been to the Philly Relays the previous year, and Artie had been there several times to see Ted compete in high school and college. They told Ed the details of what to expect.

The boys traded messages with members of the girls' team. They found out that the Green Ridge girls had run well, setting season's bests in the 4x100 relay (49.70) and 4x400 relay (4:09.04) but with over 500 teams in each of those events, they had not come close to qualifying to be one of the 36 teams in the 4x100 relay, or 18 teams in the 4x400 relay qualifying to return on Friday for the championship or consolation events.

When the vehicles arrived in West Philadelphia, they checked on the phone with Mrs. Wimble who was with the Green Ridge girls in the stadium. The girls had finished and were getting ready to leave and travel home. They needed to transfer the team packet with the stadium passes to Mr. Wimble. After parking the vehucles, Mr. Wimble, Mr. Logan, and the boys met Mrs. Wimble and the girls near the security area outside the stadium and received the team packet. Then the girls headed out.

Even though the weather was still marginal, Mr. Wimble thought it important for all the boys to see the venue to make things easier in the morning. Stadium passes in hand; they first went inside the stadium. It was huge with over 50,000 seats for the spectators. Artie knew from having previously been a spectator to see Ted run there at previous Penn Relays, it often drew a crowd of over 40,000 on Saturdays, and even sold out the year that Usain Bolt came back after his Olympic gold medals.

The boys noticed many track & field officials. Artie had purchased a glossy Philly Relays program on the way into the stadium and turned to the listing of the officials. He saw several hundred names. Ted had explained the hierarchy of hats they wore. The university colors were red and blue. Most of the officials wore red hats but the chief officials wore blue hats. There were also some assistant chief officials, and they wore green hats – green because the University was in the Ivy League. And a few officials (the meet directors, referees, and jury of appeals) wore gold hats. They were the ultimate authorities.

After seeing the stadium, Chuck brought them all down to the river fields where there were the throwing venues. He had thrown the javelin there the previous year. Artie noticed that there were even some stands for the spectators that the throwing events drew.

Near the throwing area, was a new state-of-the-art indoor track & field facility. It had cost millions to build - mostly on funds raised from the alumni. It almost put the SAC at State University to shame.

Ted had told Artie that the indoor facility was important to the Philly Relays for two reasons: First, when the weather is bad, some field events can be moved inside. Second, it was one more place to go to warm-up.

Finally, it was time to go back to the vehicles and head to the hotel. They checked in efficiently and brought their luggage upstairs. The nine boys divided into three trios: one captain and two other boys assigned to each of the rooms. Each room had double beds and a pull-out sofa bed. Artie had a room with Sean and Ed, while Bruce had a room with the Carters, leaving the third room to Chuck, Michael, and Tommy.

Everybody went to dinner, followed by a team meeting with the coaches. The High School Boys' 4x800 relay was the first event on the track on Friday scheduled to start at 9 AM. Chuck was throwing the Javelin at 10 AM outside the stadium at the throwing fields near the river. The 4x100 relay was later in the morning.

Coach Mallory always said that the human body should be awake for at least three hours before competing in a race or field event. Coach Wimble and the team agreed that wake-up call would be 6 AM for the 4x800 team and Chuck. He would take the relay team to the stadium, and Chuck to the throwing venue for those events. Mr. Logan would bring the 4x100 team later.

The boys went back to their room and sent messages, checked the latest results and news about the Philly Relays and did a little gaming but made an early night of it.

At 6 AM, the alarms went off, and the boys awoke. The hotel rooms had a small refrigerator which they had stocked with milk and juice. They had also brought some individual boxes of cereal. Artie knew he had to get some food into his stomach, but he wanted it to stay down after his race. He had found that rice cereal and skim milk together with apple juice would digest easily and not cause any problems.

After the 4x800 team and Chuck ate and dressed, they headed out with Mr. Wimble. The 4x800 team got out of the SUV near the stadium to do warm-ups while Mr. Wimble found a place to park and then headed with Chuck down to the throwing field. After Chuck checked in, Mr. Wimble headed back up to meet the 4x800 team near the competitors' entrance of the stadium.

Ted had tipped off Artie to a good place for a warmup. The four runners headed up steps on the other side of 32nd Street from the stadium and headed west on Locust Walk which bisected the college campus.

The boys headed west up the campus, nearly deserted, early in the morning. They saw a building named Town Hall at which the engineering school was located. Ted told Artie scientists built the first mainframe computer called ENIAC there. It computed missile trajectories during World War II.

They jogged further west and saw a statue of Ben Franklin. Still further west was the building for the business school where Artie's parents had met.

Eventually the boys turned around and headed back toward the stadium. When nearby, they found a place to stretch and stride. Then they met Mr. Wimble near the competitors' entrance at the beginning of a driveway that led into the stadium.

In the driveway, the boys pinned the bib letters on their uniform shirts. They were in the second section of four sections of the 4x800 races. All the bib letters for their section started with the letter "X." Green Ridge had the letters "XG." Artie quipped that it stood for Extra Good.

Next the boys changed into their running shoes with spikes. The Philly Relays allowed pin spikes (1/4") but not the full-length spikes as used on the previous cinder track. On the driveway and in the stadium to the paddock, there was carpeting to make walking on the spikes easier.

Finally, the boys took off their sweat suits and put them in a large bag that Mr. Wimble was holding. Shortly, they heard a call for their section of the 4x800 inside the stadium.

They entered a gate into a paddock after an official checked to see that they were wearing double letters beginning with "X." The paddock was divided into four rectangular sections by flagging and they milled around the back section of the paddock a couple minutes until an official told the "X" teams to move up to the third section with each team lining up in single file and the teams lining up alphabetically with "XA" next to the wall on the north side of the paddock.

Artie could hear an official with a blue hat on a platform above the paddock speaking into a microphone. He noted that two of the eighteen "X" teams were missing and called for them to report. He then told the "X" teams to move into the second section of the paddock to make more room for the "Y" teams behind them.

Next, the official turned his attention to the "W" teams who were in the front section of the paddock. He told the runners to turn and face the wall. Then he instructed the runners in each leg of the relay to exit the paddock in the front towards the track. First, the second legs headed to the exchange zone, then the first legs headed to the starting line and handed in their relay cards which had the names of their team and its runners. Next the third legs went out along the wall, and then the anchor legs.

Once the "W" teams had exited, the official called up the "X" teams to the front section and confirmed that the two missing teams were no-shows. As the race with the "W" teams was ending, the official told the "X" teams to turn and face the wall. Then the relay legs exited and as soon as the "W" race ended, Ed headed to the exchange zone, Sean to the starting line (after handing in the Green Ridge card), and Artie and Tom next to the brick wall nearby.

Quickly, the starter's pistol went off and the race began. Sean settled near the middle of the sixteen leadoff runners during the first lap and then had a nice kick on the second lap to hand the baton to Ed in fourth place.

As usual, Ed was under instructions to hang with the runner ahead of him as long as he could. After he and the other runners finished their first lap, Artie and the other third legs moved into the exchange zone according to their team's place. Artie lined up fourth from the inside until a runner passed Ed with 200-meters to go, and Artie shifted to fifth position on the exchange line.

Artie took the baton and noticed two things: the pace was quick, and even though the stadium was far less than half full this early, spectators were making more noise than he had ever heard at a meet. He held on to fifth place for the first lap when two runners passed him. However, on the back straight of the second lap, he started a long drive and coming off the last turn he caught back one of the runners to hand off the baton to Tom in sixth place.

Tommy immediately went to work – not trying to catch the runners ahead of him all at once but gradually narrowing the gap. He moved to fifth place after 300 meters, into fourth place after 600 meters, and caught up to the third-place runner with 50 meters to go. They battled during the final seconds of the race, but Tommy edged ahead to win the bronze medals for Green Ridge.

Sean, Ed, and Artie had waited for Tommy to finish and went over to embrace him. The boys exited the track and worked their way over to the seats in the grandstand on the southwest corner of the stadium where it had been pre-arranged to meet Mr. Wimble. He had their sweatsuits which they put on. They then watched the last of the four sections of the 4x800.

The Eastwood team was sitting next to Mr. Wimble, but Coach Kowalski had already gone down to the throwing fields. However, the Eastwood assistant coach had helped Mr. Wimble time the boys' relay splits: Sean (1:59.6). Ed (2:03.4), Artie (2:02.5), and Tommy (1:54.3). It added up to 7:59.83. They had broken 8 minutes – the first Green Ridge team to do so in several years.

Presently, the fourth section of the 4x800s finished and Mr. Wimble jotted down the times of the top teams from the scoreboard. He then compared notes with the Eastwood coach and announced to the boys that he had good news and bad news.

The good news was that the relay team had indeed won bronze medals by finishing third in their section and finished under 8 minutes. The bad news was that fourteen teams in the four sections had times under 8 minutes and only twelve teams qualified for the championship final on Saturday. Of those fourteen teams, Green Ridge was fourteenth. They did not qualify to run on Saturday.

The boys did not have time to be disappointed. The High School Boys Javelin was starting at 10 AM. They did their cooldown by jogging to the throwing fields outside the stadium just in time to see Chuck James in the event. Mr. Wimble followed in a walk behind them. Mr. Logan had arrived with the 4x100 relay team, which stayed behind getting ready to warm up.

CHAPTER THIRTY-FIVE
LATE APRIL
(CONTINUED)

*T*he boys arrived at the Javelin field just before the start of the event. They found out that there were eighteen throwers who would get three attempts each. At that point, the field would cut in half to nine competitors and the order rearranged from ninth place to first place for three additional attempts each.

Chuck would start off throwing fifth.

Chuck had told Artie that he thought he needed a throw over 200 feet – a distance he had been chasing for over a year. Artie also knew that at the Philly Relays, measurements were metric instead of in feet and inches.

Fortunately, Artie's Uncle Jack had given Artie a book for Christmas a couple of years ago called *The Big Gold Book*. It had lots of useful track & field information including conversion tables from metric to imperial distances. The book did not come in digital form, but Artie had taken pictures of the pages which showed conversion for every centimeter between 58 meters and 64 meters which converted to about 190 to 210 feet. The pictures were in his smart phone. Most importantly, He knew that 60.92 meters converted to 200 feet.

Chuck took his first throw which looked good and measured 59.46 meters which converted to an inch over 195 feet. At the end of the first round, he was in third place. On his second throw, Chuck fouled by stepping over the throwing line and there was no measurement taken. On his third throw, he really let loose, and it was a legal throw. Artie thought it was well over 61 meters and the official reading was 61.89 meters or exactly 203 feet. That mark put Chuck in the lead.

Artie could see college coaches intently watching Chuck throw. They had heavily recruited him. Chuck had decided early on that he did not want to go to a western college because he wanted to be closer to home. Big Ten and ACC schools had made strong pitches. Chuck finally made his decision and accepted a scholarship that would send him to the Commonwealth of Virginia – at the same university that his mom had gone to school. After a visit there, he thought it was a good academic village (as they called it) and a good place to throw the javelin.

The officials made the cut after the third round was complete. They announced the order for the remaining nine throwers to take their remaining three throws. Chuck would go last as the leader.

On his fourth throw Chuck fouled badly. His fifth throw was legal but did not improve on his best throw. Everybody watched the other eight throwers make their final attempts, but nobody could surpass 203 feet. Chuck had already won when it was time to make his final attempt. He gave it a good ride but one of his foot barely went over the line for a foul. Nevertheless, he would gladly settle for his winning throw which was finally over 200 feet.

The boys quickly congratulated Chuck and said they would see him back at the stadium for the Awards ceremony. They especially wanted to see the Philly Relays watch he had won. It was the first watch won by a Green Ridge athlete since Steve Brody was champion of the Philly Relays shot put back in Ted Stewart's day. However, the boys had to hustle back to the stadium to try to catch the Green Ridge 4x100 relay team in action.

There were over sixty trial heats (with over 500 relay teams) of the High School Boys' 4x100 taking about two hours to complete. They had been going for over an hour and a half when the boys returned to the stadium. Fortunately, the Green Ridge 4x100 team had not yet run. Shortly thereafter, the boys saw the Green Ridge team in Lane 7 in what somebody said was the 57th heat.

Realistically, Green Ridge did not have much chance at being one of the 36 relay teams to qualify for one of the four 4x100 final races on Saturday. However, they were hoping for a good showing.

Bruce crouched for the start and the starter's pistol went off. He got a good start, and the three handoffs of the baton during the lap were good, but the team was in a tough heat and could only finish sixth. However, Artie saw their time on the scoreboard was 45.10 – Green Ridge's best of the season.

Green Ridge had finished for Friday and the boys were hungry and needed to do some more jogging to cool down. So, after the 4x100 team returned to the stands and sat with Mr. Wimble, the 4x800 team jogged back up Locust Walk which became Locust Street at 40th Street and continued to 43rd Street to the deli.

At the deli, they had to wait on a short line, but the owner handed out free slices of turkey, roast beef, and cheese as samples during the wait. The sandwiches were huge, and everything was to go, so the boys started back towards the stadium until they found benches on campus to sit down and eat lunch.

After the boys returned to the stadium, they sat and watched races on the afternoon schedule including the College Distance Medley and Sprint Medley Championships, the High School Distance Medley Championships, the individual High School Miles and High School 3,000 meters championships races.

There was also Chuck's Award ceremony on the infield. Afterwards, Chuck came up to the stands and showed off his Philly Relays watch. And Mr. Wimble gave the 4x800 team their bronze medals which he had picked up.

The Philly Relays schedule would continue with distance races into the evening. But Mr. Wimble said it was time to return to the hotel and get dinner.

Dinner was good and there was another team meeting afterwards. On Saturday, they only had Sean in the race walk, and the 4x400 relay team. The boys went back to their rooms. Artie spoke to his parents on his phone. They had seen his race and congratulated him on the medal. They had just been to dinner with Mr. and Mrs. Fisher. Artie then sent out some messages and played some games on his phone, but he was tired and went to bed early and fell asleep quickly.

The race walks were from 7 AM to 8:45 AM on Saturday at the Philly Relays. Sean was in the Men's U20 division – "U20" stands for under 20-years old. The race was set for 7:30 AM, which meant the wake-up call for Sean was at the early time of 4:30 AM. Artie and Ed got an extra hour of shut-eye and awakened at 5:30 AM to accompany Sean to the stadium.

Because the race walk event was not a high school event (as it also included young college students), Sean would wear a Strider shirt and the Strider race walking coach picked the three boys up and brought them to the stadium.

At the stadium, Artie found out that the U20 men were competing at the same time as the Open Men and Masters Men, although there were separate awards for each division.

There were only eight U20 Men in the race and Sean knew some of them from the Junior Olympics and other previous competitions. The race began and the Strider coach began taking time splits for Sean at each lap and each kilometer. The coach read the times and Artie recorded them on paper on a clipboard.

There are two basic rules in the racewalk: (1) one foot must always be on the ground to the visible eye, and (2) the walker's knee must lock as the leg comes back in the stride. In shorthand, the walker must not engage in lifting or creeping.

There were judges around the track holding warning cards and red cards. If a walker was close to a violation, a judge would wave a warning card at him. A red card was a violation and if three judges gave red cards, a walker was disqualified or in some races put in a penalty box for a time.

Artie could tell the competitors in the U20 division because they were wearing bib numbers 50 to 59. Although there were adult competitors ahead of Sean, Artie could see that Sean was the early leader among the U20 competitors.

Artie could also see that Sean was not receiving red cards and had only one warning. Sean had told him that the Strider walk coach was a stickler for good form. That really paid off in big events when the judging was usually tighter than local competitions.

Sean's lap times looked impressive. Artie thought about cross-country times for a 5K race. Runners who did a 5K in 16 or 17 minutes were good, and even 18 or 19 minutes were respectable. Sean was on pace to finish under 23 minutes *walking!* Very impressive!

Sean clicked off his remaining laps to finish first among the U20 walkers in a time of 22:52.8. For the second time in two days, Artie would get to see a Philly Relays watch.

After the Awards Ceremony, the group of four were all hungry and they exited the stadium and found a place nearby to get egg sandwiches, tea, and coffee. They next returned to the stadium.

At the stadium, Mr. Wimble and Mr. Logan had arrived with the rest of the Green Ridge team. Sean showed off his Philly Relays watch, and everyone viewed the early sections of the high school 4x400s.

There would be over forty sections of the 4x400s with over 500 teams that would take over three hours of the schedule. For over two hours, there would be "unclassified" sections with a mix of teams from various states and the Caribbean. These sections started with slower teams and got faster as the day went on. During the last hour of the 4x400s, there were "classified" sections which included only teams from various parts of the Philadelphia metropolitan area.

The Green Ridge team was not as fast as in recent years, but the school's reputation caused it to be in a faster section than it deserved at 11 AM. After watching the early relay sections, the four runners on the Green Ridge relay team left the stands to warm up.

In the early sections, the winning teams had times over 3:30 but as the sections continued, the winning times dropped under 3:30.

Green Ridge's time today was important for one big reason. A team had to finish under 3:40 or else it was put on probation – meaning it would have to sit out from running the 4x400 in the following year. Barring an injury or dropped baton, Green Ridge expected to finish well under 3:40.

Eventually, Mr. Wimble left the stands to meet the relay team and help them check in. A while later, Artie could see the Green Ridge team in the paddock, and then at the starting line as one of fifteen teams in their race.

The start was a jumble, but Tommy stayed on his feet and handed off the baton after a lap. He was exactly in the middle of the pack. The Carter cousins lost ground in the middle relay legs, and Michael Thomas gained ground on the anchor leg.

Artie saw a time of 3:32.42 for Green Ridge on the scoreboard. He saw on Mr. Wimble's clipboard that Tommy and Michael had run in the 52s, and the Carter cousins in the 53s.

The competitive day for Green Ridge was complete but the team stayed to watch big afternoon events. During the 2 PM to 4 PM timeslot, the meet was live on national television and there were various events with Olympic athletes and college championship events. The biggest crowd pleaser, however, was the 100 meter dash for men over the age of 85 years old.

After 4 PM, the team stayed a while longer to see the College 4x800 championships, and the High School Boys 4x800 and 4x400 championships. Then, even though the meet had another hour to wind down, it was time for the Green River squad to depart to get home at a reasonable hour.

On the ride back to Meadow County, Artie looked at the printed program he had purchased and his bronze medal. The program even had his name in it as part of the 4x800 relay team! It had been a good weekend. Now it was time to focus on the upcoming meets in May.

CHAPTER THIRTY-SIX: EARLY MAY

Green Ridge had a 2-2 record in dual and tri-meets with three NEIL opponents yet to face: third-seeded Overlook on the first May Wednesday, and second-seeded Meadow Regional plus last-seeded Undercliff on the second May Wednesday as rescheduled after the postponement caused by the storm in early April.

Green Ridge had no worries about defeating Undercliff, but it would need an upset to defeat either of their better seeded opponents. Losing to them both would cause the unthinkable: Green Ridge with a losing record in the league standings, something that had never happened in Bill Mallory's entire tenure as coach.

Artie discussed the situation on the phone with Ted while Ted was taking a break from studying for his final exams at law school. Ted thought the lineup against Overlook was set but less certain against the Meadow Regional.

"You might want to switch a couple teammates among events against the Larks. I have an idea," said Ted.

"And what might that be?" responded Artie.

"We really need to know what the Larks have depth-wise. I think I will call a few of my alumni friends to be 'spies' at the Meadow-Riverside dual meet this Wednesday. At least, one of them can watch the track events, one can cover the jumps, and one can cover the throws. With more information, you can make better decisions."

"Okay," gulped Artie. "But is it legal to do that?"

"Perfectly legal," chuckled Ted. "The meets are open to the public. In fact, there has been 'spying' at various times in the past by both Green Ridge and Riverside on each other," answered Ted. "Coaches Mallory and Flynn have always taken it in stride. In fact, sometimes they have asked the spies if they want to help time the track events or help record the field event marks."

The weather was good on Wednesday. Artie expected the meet with Overlook to be close and it was. In the first twelve events, each team won six of them: Green Ridge in the 110 hurdles, triple jump, high jump, Mile, 800, and javelin, while Overlook won the 100 meters, the 400 meters, the 400-meter hurdles, pole vault, shot put, and discus.

Green Ridge had one bad break in the early going. Sam Carter twisted his ankle badly landing on his first triple jump attempt. Artie had hoped Sam could score points in the jumps and/or the 200-meter dash. Instead of Green Ridge having a narrow lead, there was a tie score of 54-54 going into the final four events.

Green Ridge now needed 16 points to tie or 17 points to win from the four events – the 3,000 meters, the 200 meters, the long jump, and the 4x400 relay. In the 3,000 meters, Artie and Ed easily took the top two places to give Green Ridge a temporary lead, but with Sam Carter injured, Overlook came right back and took the top two places in the 200 meters to tie the meet again, this time by a 63-63 score.

Either team could now win the meet by winning the top two places in the long jump worth eight points. Otherwise, the winner of the relay would win the meet.

Bruce Griffin took the lead in the long jump on his first attempt and needed no more. But with Sam Carter out of the picture, Overlook easily took second and third place. The score was 68-67 with five points from the relay still up for grabs.

With the meet on the line, Tommy was a quick addition to the relay team, as well as a sophomore replacing Sam Carter. On the first two legs, Overlook built up a twenty meter lead. Tommy chased on the third leg and cut the lead in half. Michael Thomas chased some more and made it close but could not catch the Overlook anchor leg.

Final score: Overlook 72, Green Ridge 68.

That evening, Artie received the reports from alumni about the Meadow-Riverside dual meet. At least he knew exactly what they would be facing next week.

The Green Ridge team had a whole week to think about the heartbreaking loss to Overlook and get ready for the showdown with Meadow Regional. This was because Buddy McGurk had not scheduled the team to attend an invitational meet on the first weekend in May as they usually did.

Fortunately, there was something to pick up the spirits of Artie and his cohorts. On Friday afternoon, the senior class had its last outing: a picnic at County Park.

It was fun. The school provided box lunches for the seniors and there were picnic tables. There were also other things to do.

The county zoo (with North American animals) was open and always interesting. There was also a kid-sized train which circled around the zoo. Most students had ridden it years ago and were nostalgic to ride it again. There was also a carousel which was still operating, and students wanted to ride it again too.

The park also had various sporting venues. The varsity athletes could not participate because of the risk of injury, but they could officiate, coach, or merely observe.

Certain students brought their tennis rackets and headed to the tennis courts.

Other students brought basketballs and went to the outdoor basketball courts. They could just shoot the ball around or play three on three.

There were also softball fields, and a slow-pitch game started up. Not everybody had brought gloves but there were enough to lend to each other.

Artie and Debbie, however, just wanted to have a nice leisurely long walk together. There was much to talk about: the rest of the track & field season, the upcoming prom, and graduation.

The good news was that the State University had also accepted Debbie and she had decided to go there. They still would be seeing plenty of each other during the next school year.

Artie had already talked to Tommy O'Leary (who was also going to State University) and they were planning on being college roommates. None of Debbie's teammates were going to State University, and she was looking at other options for a roommate.

Debbie, however, had one edge on Artie. She was all set on what she wanted for a major: She hoped to teach Special Education when she finished college. Artie, on the other hand, was very undecided about a college major.

Yes, their high school experience was quickly heading to its conclusion. But new horizons were ahead.

CHAPTER THIRTY-SEVEN: MID MAY

Ted Stewart finished his last exam of the semester at the law school on Monday and was back home on Monday night, reviewing all the details of the results of the Meadow-Riverside dual meet. Then he sat down with Artie:

"I can see three things that you ought to consider for Wednesday."

"Go ahead."

"First, with Sam Carter out with the ankle sprain, we need another guy in the 200 meters. Michael Thomas is the guy even if he will be tired for the relay. We do not have much chance in the relay anyway."

"Yeah. In the 200 meters, we only have two of the six lanes in the first section because it is a tri-meet. So, we put him with Jeff Carter there?"

Ted thought about it for a second and remembered a dual meet when he was on the team.

"Let another soph run in the first section with Jeff and have Mike run in the second section. We might catch them off guard."

"What else?"

"We also lost Sam in the long jump. Anybody who might be a second scorer there?"

"We don't have any sophs over 18 feet, but there is one frosh jumper - Tim Lamar."

Ted chuckled. "He has a good personal coach. Might as well try it."

"Anything else?"

"I saved the best for last. The only way I can see us winning the meet is to take first and second in all three distance events."

"Because league rules forbid tripling in the distance events, Sean and Tommy have been doing the Mile and 800 meters all season while Ed and I have stuck to the 3,000 meters."

"I know, but if you remember from cross-country, their top two distance guys are really half-milers and kickers. I am confident that Tommy and Sean can beat them in the Mile, but they might be able to split our guys up in the 800 meters."

"What can we do about that?"

"The way I figure it, they are going to hope for a slow pace in the Mile to save themselves for the 800 meters. If the Mile pace is fast, it will take the starch out of their legs. But better not to have Sean or Tommy to do the work setting a quick pace. I do not think you can score in the Mile, but being a fast pacesetter could help the team. And I think you would still have enough left for the 3,000 meters."

"Consider it done. Let me send messages to Sean and Tommy about these adjustments."

Wednesday turned out to have beautiful weather: low 70s, partly sunny, and little wind.

The buses from Meadow Regional and Undercliff arrived after the school day with their teams. Artie almost felt sorry for the Undercliff team. The Larks and Knights would virtually ignore them this afternoon while focused on each other. Undercliff's realistic goal was at least to score in the low-double digits against both opponents.

Artie noticed that Meadow Regional had brought quite a contingent. Afterall, it was the last meet of the year for the Junior Varsity athletes. He especially noticed a plethora of throwers with them.

He had heard they had a new assistant coach who had revitalized their throwing program.

The Meadow Head Coach was Al Nimmo. He had never beaten Green Ridge in a track & field dual meet. Last year, his team (although favored) could only salvage a 70-70 tie. He was optimistic that this was the year that Meadow Regional would finally achieve a victory over Green Ridge.

The meet started off well as Bruce edged out Meadow's star hurdler in a swing event. Next, Jeff Carter took second in the 100 meters.

In the Mile, Sean, Tommy and Artie and Meadow's top two distance runners quickly separated themselves from the rest of the field. Artie took the lead and forced the pace for three laps like a rabbit. After the bell, the other four runners passed him, and he just eased to the finish. Sean and Tommy took the top two spots giving Green Ridge an early 16-11 lead.

Next up on the track were the 400 meter run and 400 meter hurdles. Michael Thomas could not run the 400 meters and the 400m hurdles back-to-back. Jeff Carter would run the former, and Michael would run the latter.

Jeff was the only hope for Green Ridge to prevent a sweep in the 400 meters. He had a good start and stayed close to the two Overlook opponents in the first section but could not beat either of them. His time bested all the times in the second section, and he earned a valuable point for third place.

The first section of the 400 meter hurdles next went to the line. Michael Thomas was close to Meadow's star hurdler for the first half of the race but ran out of gas. He finished second for three points.

Results from the field events finally started coming in. The best that Green Ridge could do in the Pole Vault was third place. The Javelin was finally complete. Chuck won it with a single throw, but the Larks took second and third place. The Larks now led by a 37-26 score.

The 800 meters was next up on the track. Tommy took out the first lap hard, and the Mile race had taken its toll on the Meadow distance duo. Tommy and Sean easily outkicked them to finish in the top two spots. More news came in on the field events: Bruce had won the triple jump. The Lark's lead had narrowed to a 42-39 score.

The Green Ridge boys and girls made sure that every available Junior Varsity and Frosh entered the 800 meters to make it last as long as possible. After six sections of the 800 meters, the 200-meter dash finally started. Michael Thomas had plenty of rest from his earlier race. In the first section of the 200 meters, the top sprinter for the Larks beat Jeff Carter with a winning time of 22.9 seconds. The rest of the field trailed by a wide margin.

Michael Thomas was in Lane 4 of the second section of the 200 meter dash. He seemed confident and felt loose after his previous race. Plus, this was his short race. A piece of cake! He got off to an excellent start and had a clear lead coming into the straight. He turned on the jets, driving hard right past the finish line. Everybody held their breaths until the timers read their times. Michael had run a time of 22.8 seconds and pulled an upset to win the event! The score was now a 45-45 tie.

Artie went to the starting line for the 3,000 meter run with Ed Glavine. If they won the event, Green Ridge would finally take the lead. And they were only facing Meadow's third and fourth best distance runners.

The first mile was at a middling pace, but Artie did not want to leave matters to chance so he picked things up on the fifth lap and Ed followed him. They broke contact with the Meadow runners.

The sixth lap was okay, and Artie had a considerable lead. Then on the back straight of the final lap, it hit him. The fast pacesetting in the Mile had taken a toll. His legs began to feel like rubber, and he was slowing down. On the last turn, Ed pulled up alongside him and hesitated.

"Go!" Artie gasped. "Go!"

Ed took off into the last straight towards the finish line. Artie just tried to keep moving. Everything seemed in slow motion. He could hear noise from the crowd which meant the Meadow runners must be narrowing the gap. Finally, he leaned into the finish line and fell to the track just beyond the line as the Meadow runners went past him moments too late.

More field events were complete. Bruce had won his third event – the high jump – and Chuck was runner-up in the shot put. Green Ridge now had a narrow 61-56 lead with the long jump, the discus – which was starting late – and the 4x400 relay to go.

Green Ridge needed nine points to tie (70-70) or at least ten points to win (71-69) the meet. Absent a dropped baton, they were unlikely to get any points in the relay. Sean went over to watch the discus while Artie stayed at the long jump area next to the track.

The jumpers each got 4 attempts. In the first round, Bruce had an almost perfect jump that measured exactly 21 feet and took a commanding lead. The best Meadow jumper hit 19'10." Then there was a big drop off. The next best Meadow jumper registered an 18'2.5" jump. The next best Knight was surprisingly a frosh jumper - Tim Lamar – with a 17'9" jump.

In the second round, nobody improved: the two Meadow athletes fouled, and Bruce and Tim did not exceed their first attempts. In the third round, again nobody improved. This time, Bruce and Tim fouled, and the Meadow jumpers failed to do better.

The jumpers made their final attempts. Bruce improved to 21'6" and the Meadow top jumper improved to 20"1.5."

Next up was Tim Lamar. He ran down the runway and hit the takeoff board perfectly. There was quiet until the jump measured 18'4" and then cheers. Tim had moved into third place and every point mattered.

The pressure was now on Meadow's second jumper. He ran down the runway but stepped two inches past the take-off board – a foul on his final attempt.

Six big points for Green Ridge gave them a 67-59 lead temporarily but Meadow Regional easily won the relay to narrow it to a 67-64 score with just the discus left. Artie hustled over to the discus area. The one extra point that Tim Lamar gained in the Long Jump meant that Chuck now needed only second place in the discus to earn a tie in the meet 70-70.

But the news from the discus was not encouraging. As usual, the event was Chuck's nemesis. Doing the spin always seemed to give him trouble. He had fouled on his first attempt while the three top opposing throws had marks of 147'3," "138"6," and 128"9."

On his second attempt, Chuck took a "safety" throw to get on the board with a 138'3" mark. That moved him into third place, which would be good for a point which would not be enough. Green Ridge needed at least three points in the discus to gain a tie and finish the dual meet season 3-3-1 to avoid a losing season. Chuck needed to improve his best discus throw of the day by at least four inches.

On his third attempt, Chuck fouled badly. He was still having trouble with his spin. Fortunately, none of the Meadow throwers improved on their best marks. It all came down to Chuck's final attempt.

Artie told Chuck about the extra point in the Long Jump and that if Chuck could even get four more inches on his last throw, Green Ridge could get a tie against Meadow Regional and avoid a losing record. That relaxed Chuck a little. Four more inches seemed far easier than nine more feet.

Chuck went into the discus circle for his final throw and began his spin around and around. It looked like he might land outside the circle again, but after teetering a bit he stayed in the circle. It was a legal throw if it landed in the sector. The disc arced in the air higher and higher. The sun rays from the lowering sun in the sky glinted off the rim of the disc into the eyes of the spectators. Then, the disc began to descend lower and lower – until it hit the ground just past 150 feet in the middle of the sector. First place was even better than second place! Five big points for Green Ridge!

The final score: Green Ridge 72, Meadow Regional 68.

Green Ridge had also defeated Undercliff 128-12. They finished with a winning record of 4-3. And the Green Ridge Girl's team won a double victory to finish with a 4-3 record as well.

The Meadow's coach Al Nimmo shook his head wistfully. He would have to wait another year to try and defeat the Knights.

CHAPTER THIRTY-EIGHT: MID MAY (CONTINUED)

Hours after the tri-meet, Artie learned that Spring Valley had upset Eastwood (which had suffered late season injuries) in their final dual meet.

In the final NEIL dual meet standings for the boys' teams, Riverside was 7-0, Meadow Regional was 5-2, and Green Ridge, Overlook, and Eastwood, all tied at 4-3. This meant that the league meet would decide which of the three teams would get the third seed next year for scheduling purposes.

The Green Ridge girls' team had won third place outright in their standings with a 5-2 record. The frosh teams had also done well. The frosh boys were undefeated as they had been in cross-country. The frosh girls were 5-2 matching the varsity girls. No scores were kept for the junior varsity in track & field unlike cross-country.

Artie liked the Green Ridge's boys chances of snagging the third seed. Track & field is the opposite of cross country in one respect. In cross country, three stars can carry a team to victory in a dual meet, but a team needs more depth to do well in a larger meet. In track & field, a team needs depth for a dual meet, but its stars can be the key in a larger championship meet.

Such proved to be the case in the NEIL championships on Saturday. Bruce Griffin won two gold and two silver medals to score 36 points. Chuck easily won the Javelin for another ten points, and

Sean, Tommy, Artie, and Ed scored an additional 34 points in the three distance events including Tommy's victory in the 800 meters. Ed edged Artie out again in the 3,000 meters as they finished in fourth and fifth place.

The above added up to 80 points in eight events from just six athletes and the Green Knights managed to gather another 12 points – three more points from Chuck in the shot and discus, and nine points from other athletes to finish with 92 points behind Riverside (120) and Meadow Regional (97) but easily ahead of Overlook (70) and Eastwood (54). The other teams trailed: Spring Valley (49), Arcola (10), and Undercliff (4).

On Sunday afternoon, Coach Mallory invited the four captains and Ed Glavine for a visit.

Ted was already there when the boys arrived in the living room of the Mallory home. Coach Mallory was in a wheelchair with someone that Artie guessed was a nurse or aide.

Artie tried not to show shock at the sight of Coach Mallory. He had lost all his hair and a lot of weight. But his handshake was firm, and his voice was steady.

"Gentlemen, sit down, sit down. I am so proud of your efforts this week. I can just imagine the look on Al Nimmo's face when the meet with Meadow Regional ended," chuckled Mallory.

He continued: "I did not get a chance to tell you, Ted, that earlier today Sonny Lamar stopped by at my invitation. I want to thank you for accepting him with open arms. Not only did his coaching the long jumpers get us that critical extra point, but it helped me bring the matter of Sonny Lamar to closure. I always felt bad how things ended. I now know that he learned his lesson and he apologized to me. He has turned into a good adult."

"By the way, I also spoke to Tommy earlier. He is at a family baptism this afternoon."

Mallory next asked for many details about the tri-meet and league meet, He had clearly looked over the results online closely. He enjoyed every minute of the discussion. Then he got serious for a few minutes.

"And you must be Ed Glavine," said the Coach pointing at Ed.

"Yes, sir!" answered Ed Glavine.

"Well, you are having a mighty fine sophomore year. Next year, I expect you will be the top runner on the cross country team. And in two years, you may be the captain. I hope the examples of these four captains rub off on you. The best of luck."

"Thank you very much."

"Now as for you captains!"

"First, Chuck. You have an Olympic dream to chase. It will take all your talent, hard work, perseverance, and some luck, but you have a chance. Take it and get a good education as well for your post-athletic career."

"Sean, you also have an Olympic dream to chase but a far different road to take. The NCAA does not have race walking as an event, but the NAIA does. You are smart to go to an NAIA track & field program that has race walkers and a coach who knows the event."

"Keep in mind that there are fewer competitive walkers in our sport than the other events, but the USA typically only qualifies one man at most for the Olympic 20K race walk compared to three in most other events.

"Of course, the World Track & Field Championships also has the 20K walk and the USA sends a whole team of walkers to the Race Walking World Cup. Simply getting on a USA team to an international competition would be a huge achievement. Your first opportunity will be going to the USATF U20 meet for under 20-year olds in late June which qualifies for the World U20 meet. They have a 10K for the race walk distance."

Coach Mallory next turned to Bruce.

"Bruce, choosing an NCAA Division 2 school is an excellent decision. You should be extremely competitive in the hurdles and jumps with a chance to qualify for Nationals. You may even have the alternative of becoming a good decathlete if you decide to learn the pole vault!"

"And Artie, I hope you consider running on the State University team. I know Tommy has also committed to State University. I said to him earlier and to you now, that I think you would make good roommates. I also think your talents may really lie in the Steeplechase and 10,000 meters. I would like you and Ted to visit me after your season is over to talk about it some more."

"Anyway, Gentlemen, I want to congratulate you. You have done the Green Ridge Knights proud in difficult circumstances. But it is time for my daily afternoon medications which may put me to sleep. So, we will have to cut this visit short. Please offer my congratulations and best wishes to the rest of the team as well."

With that, the boys departed as the nurse or aide was giving Coach Mallory pills and had a shot to give him as well.

CHAPTER THIRTY-NINE: LATE MAY

The Meadow County Championships the following week were a wash-out, or at least half a washout. Early events were on Friday afternoon in dry weather, but the bulk of the meet on Saturday was in the rain.

With all said and done, Green Ridge finished in fourth place behind Riverside, Fairmont (the top 4A school), and Meadow Regional. Tommy O'Leary, Chuck James, and Bruce Griffin (in the Long Jump) won three gold medals while the full team pulled in 52 points. Ed Glavine edged Artie in the 3,000 meters for the third time in a row. Artie reluctantly realized that he might never defeat Ed at that distance again. The protégé had surpassed the mentor.

When Ted and Artie returned home from the meet, their parents told them to sit down and gave them the news that Coach Mallory had just passed away. It had been a long time since Artie had cried about anything, but he broke down in tears. Mrs. Stewart consoled him, while Mr. Stewart consoled Ted.

The next day the arrangements were in the obituary. There would be a wake at the funeral home from 4 PM to 8 PM on Wednesday and a funeral at the church at 10 AM on Thursday.

The captains sent messages to each other and agreed that the team should send some flowers to the wake, preferably with green and white carnations representing the school colors. They would ask team members to chip in a few bucks each. The captains would chip in a bit more. Mrs. Stewart helped Artie order the flowers from a local florist online.

The school made plans to bring the teams to the wake and funeral in school buses. Because the expectations were a big crowd at the wake, the school got an okay to bring the buses to the funeral home after school ahead of the public at about 3:30 PM to pay their respects.

The captains led the team into the lobby in the funeral home where they signed the guestbook. Then they went into the next room where they saw a receiving line of Coach Mallory's family and the casket.

First, they paid their respects to Mrs. Mallory who thanked them for providing information about the team all year allowing her to keep the team page on social media active.

Next on the receiving line were the Coach's four daughters and their husbands, and then the grandchildren. Artie talked to one of the husbands who happened to be his older cousin – Uncle Jack's son. He, in turn, introduced Artie to a grandson named John who was going to the state Junior Olympics next month.

Artie got in a conversation with young John who said he had tried various track & field events and liked them all. He had not yet decided which three events to enter at the Junior Olympics. He really wanted to try the pole vault but was not yet old enough since the 13- & 14-year-old age group is the youngest allowed to compete in the event.

Artie asked young John if he had ever heard of the "combined" events or "multi-events" as the rule book used to call them. John said that Grandpa Mallory had mentioned them, but he did not know much about them. Artie explained that in a combined event, an athlete competes in multiple events and scores points on how well he does in each event. At the end of the events, the total points determine the winners of the medals.

Artie said that for John's age group, the combined event had three events - a triathlon with the shot put, high jump, and 400 meter dash. John seemed interested and said he would check it out.

Once the captains finished going through the receiving line they went to the casket. It was a closed casket given Coach Mallory's bad physical condition from the cancer at the end. However, there was a nice picture of Coach on top of the casket. Artie said a prayer and moved to the next room.

In the second room, there were pictures and memorabilia from Coach Mallory's decades at Green Ridge. There were team trophies borrowed from the school. There were also plaques from the various times that Coach Mallory had won Coach of the Year honors, and also newspaper articles in frames and photocopies of the track & field pages of school yearbooks in a big three-ring binder.

Artie noticed a picture of Coach Mallory and the 4x400 team including his brother that clinched a state championship. His parents had taken him to see that race as a youngster. Next to the picture was the gold-colored baton that the relay team had used on that day.

At 4 PM, the public started arriving. Among the first were Ted and some of his teammates. When they came into the second room, Ted and Artie started making introductions between Ted's teammates and Artie's teammates.

First, they introduced Steve Brody to Chuck James and the two throwers compared their Philly Relay watches. Next, they introduced Mac Callahan to Tommy O'Leary who had broken Mac's school record in the 800 meters. But they did not have to introduce Josh Johnson to Bruce Griffin since they had already met last fall. Josh and Bruce immediately started to talk about hurdling.

Artie also saw Larry Lamar mingling with his ex-teammates. All was forgiven.

Eventually, older track & field alumni started arriving. A number of alums made it a point to meet the captains in the second room and express appreciation for their efforts during a difficult season. Artie also recognized Judge Hanley from the New Year Eve parties. Judge Hanley pulled Ted aside and they talked in a corner of the room.

People kept coming and going throughout the wake. It dawned on Artie just how important Coach Mallory and his program had been to so many people. He really had a major impact on many lives during his tenure.

Finally, there was a prayer service conducted by the pastor from the church and the Knights of Columbus also said a few words about their brother Knight.

Afterwards, the bus took team members back to school except those whose parents were taking them home directly from the funeral home.

The next morning there was the funeral at the church at 10 AM. Again, there were school buses to take the teams there. They were early. The front rows of pews at the church on the right belonged to the Mallory family and relatives. The front rows on the left belonged to team members with school faculty next, then track & field alumni, and coaches and officials from the county and beyond after that. Artie noticed Coaches Kowalski, Flynn, and Nimmo, among others.

Everybody waited quietly and eventually the hearse pulled up in front of the church. Pallbearers (all track & field alumni) took the casket out of the hearse, up the steps, into the church, and down the aisle and right by the front rows in the center aisle.

It seemed to Artie that, on the one hand, it was a very solemn occasion. People were incredibly sad. On the other hand, as the priest said, it was also a celebration of a wonderful life. One of the readings that a lector read was from the Second Letter of Paul to Timothy and it particularly moved Artie:

> *The time of my departure is at hand. I have competed well. I have finished the race. I have kept the faith. From now on the crown of righteousness awaits me …*

Artie thought that those words were about perfect applied to Coach Mallory. It was amazing to see all the lives he had touched for the better. He truly had a great long run over the decades. He had to think that the Coach was up above now and keeping an eye on the team.

The pastor gave a homily after the Gospel which seemed especially comforting to the Mallory family.

After the communion service, there were eulogies about Coach Mallory. Three people spoke: a grandchild (young John), a daughter (John's mom, Judy), and Ted – representing all the Coach's athletes, or as the Pastor said, all the "sons" of Bill Mallory. All the eulogies had the congregation smiling and reminiscing. It really was truly a time to celebrate as well as to grieve.

First young John and Judy, his mom, went up to the pulpit. There was a step stool on which John stood. He spoke first and certainly was precocious. The big crowd did not scare him a bit.

John told everybody that he loved his grandpa and especially liked going to visit him and Grandma every year for the egg hunt in their backyard on Easter Sunday. He also said that Grandpa told him all about track & field and that he could hardly wait to go to the Junior Olympics next month. The last time that he saw Grandpa he told him that if he won any medals, he would give them to him as a present. Now, he would give them to Grandma to hold until she got to see Grandpa in Heaven.

John's mom Judy, who was one of Coach Mallory's daughters, next took over the microphone from John. She noted with a smile that John was a chip off the old block from his grandfather, afraid of nothing and never at a loss for words. She also noted that her father had all daughters and then a couple of granddaughters. He loved them all dearly but when John finally came along, he had Grandpa wrapped around his little finger.

Judy also told the audience about growing up in the Mallory household. Her father could have a stern exterior, but they all knew that he was really a softie inside.

Finally, Ted spoke for all Coach Mallory's athletes. He noted that Coach Mallory was always concerned about life lessons. He wanted his team to grow as people into good adults as well as to grow into good athletes. The alumni proved this by how they had gone on to successful careers and becoming outstanding members of the community - and being good husbands and fathers. He said that while Coach Mallory never had any biological sons, he had hundreds of spiritual ones, including those that were there today.

After the eulogy, School Superintendent Taft went to the podium to announce that the School Board had approved naming the track at Green Ridge in honor of Coach Mallory. They were also renaming the driveway that led to the track as "Mallory Way." He had told this to the Coach while Mallory was alive, but they had delayed the ceremony hoping he would recover and be able to attend. More details to be forthcoming.

The funeral was over, and cars began lining up to form a procession to the cemetery followed by a luncheon for family and friends. However, the teams could not attend those events. They boarded the school bus to head back to school.

CHAPTER FORTY: JUNE

Artie went to his room and collapsed on his bed. He was tired. He had finished his last final exam in high school that afternoon. There were a few days until the graduation ceremony but otherwise his high school days were over.

His high school athletic career had ended weeks ago. At the district meet, he had missed qualifying for the State Classified Championships by one place in the 3,000 meters. Ed had finished ahead of him again and qualified.

Artie was happy for Ed. It was a valuable experience for a sophomore to go to the State meet. Only four other members of the team had qualified. Chuck easily won the Javelin, Tommy won the 800 meters, Sean was fifth in the Mile, and Bruce was third, fourth, and fifth in the Long Jump, Hurdles, and High Jump, respectively.

Because Artie was a team captain, he went to the State Classified meet to cheer for his teammates. Sean and Ed did not qualify for the State All-Star Championships. It was just as well for Sean, as he could now focus on his race walking and prepare for the USATF U20 meet later in the month.

Chuck, Tommy, and Bruce were qualifiers for the State All-Star meet. Chuck won the Class 3A Javelin, Tommy was second in the 800 meters, and Bruce took a pair of Fifth Places in the Hurdles and Long Jump.

At the All-Star meet, Chuck completed his undefeated season with a throw of 205"11, a new personal and school record. Tommy was third in the 800 meters in 1:54.08 which was also a personal and school record. Bruce also had a personal best in the long jump (22' 5") to snag sixth place.

Artie pondered all this while lying on his bed. It had been a long season for him personally. And things had just petered out for him in the end. It reminded him of a line from a poem by T.S. Eliot that he had studied in English class:

This is how the world ends,

Not with a bang but a whimper.

Right now, Artie just wanted rest. Just then there was a knock on his door.

Ted came in. He had already started a summer clerkship job with a local law firm.

"Do you want to hear the big news today at the county courthouse?" asked Ted.

"Go right ahead."

'Buddy McGurk was arrested today and charged with trafficking in illegal drugs and fraud."

Artie looked amazed. Finally, he asked: "What exactly did he do?"

"According to the criminal complaint filed against him, he was feeding Performance Enhancing Drugs (PEDs) to his football players with the assistance of his offensive and defensive coordinators. To pay for the drugs, he was approving fake invoices through the athletic department for payment into bank accounts he controlled."

"How did they catch him?"

"One of his former athletes, still hooked on painkillers in college, took an overdose and almost died. He confessed to the college police who then tipped off our local police officers."

"Wow!"

"It gets better. A detective for the county police who specializes in drug cases used to throw the shot put for Green Ridge. He knew that

Coach Mallory hated PEDs and contacted him. Having been an interim Athletic Director at Green Ridge, Coach Mallory knew just where to look in the AD office and on its computer. He gave the detective an investigatory roadmap."

Ted continued.

"In late March on a Friday as school was letting out, the police, including a forensic specialist, entered the school with a search warrant. They spent much of the weekend going through the athletic department records. Armed with what they found, the District Attorney presented evidence to a grand jury dealing in drug matters. The police also questioned the offensive and defensive coordinators who eventually decided to cooperate in exchange for leniency."

"I was wondering why I had not seen McGurk the last couple months."

"In a closed session, the school board quietly suspended him in April pending what came out of the investigation. Darren Logan has been silently acting as athletic director since then. I think he will get the permanent job."

"Well, that is good news. He seemed like a good guy on the trip to the Philly Relays. And he does coach an Olympic sport. But who are going to be the track & field coaches? Mr. Wimble said he might stay on as a faculty adviser to the team, and he wants to become a track & field official. But he told already us that he and Mrs. Wimble will not be the coaches again."

"There is a three-part answer to that."

"I am game. Go ahead."

"The first part is that the injuries finally caught up with Sue. She is calling quits to her elite career on the track. She still wants to try running one or two marathons, but she does not need to be on the West Coast to train for that, so she is moving back to Meadow County."

"That's good news."

"Yes, and she has accepted a job as a history teacher at Green Ridge and will be the head cross country coach for both the girls and boys."

"That is even better news. And I hope she will coach the track & field season as well…"

"I should also mention that Sue and I have made it official, and she is now wearing an engagement ring. We have not set a date yet, but we want you to be the best man."

"That is the best news of all. Do I start calling her "Sis" now?'

Ted smiled. "Now for the second part of the answer. Before he passed away, Coach Mallory was busy talking to a bunch of people including me. I promised him that if Sue were the track coach for the girls, I'd temporarily coach the boys."

"But what about law school?"

"There an old saying among law students that in the first year, they scare you to death, the second year they work you to death, and the third year, they bore you to death. Anyway, I figure I can take a course overload in the fall semesters allowing me to an easier course load in the spring semesters with no late afternoon courses. And Sue can cover for me during final exams. We can make it work. Another law student is currently a graduate assistant for the college team."

"So how long did you promise Coach Mallory to do this?"

"Four years. I have two more years to get the law degree, and I might take a third year to get a Masters in Tax Law – but am more likely to do that later at night. And I can be a law clerk for Judge Hanley for a year or two with flexible hours - provided I get my work done. I will come to work early and leave for track practice. But I am only going to be a caretaker for the team for four years."

"Why four years?"

"Coach Mallory knew, and I know that I can certainly administer Green Ridge's track & field program, prepare workouts, and analyze what needs doing. However, my long-term talents are elsewhere. I hope to be a top official and active on the Striders club and the USATF State Association. They already asked me to be their counsel once I pass the bar exam."

"So, what is the third part of the answer?"

"Coach Mallory was convinced someone else was the candidate to take over the program for the long run. And he convinced Principal Henson and Mr. Logan who that is. The candidate that he proposed is you."

Artie was even more dumbfounded. Finally, he spoke:

"And I thought all I had to think about right now was whether I could and should run on the college team at State University."

"Coach Mallory took care of that too. He knew that it is difficult for a male walk-on to get on many college teams these days. However, he talked to the coaches at State University."

"And?"

"For decades, Green Ridge has sent athletes to their program. – I am a good example. The college coaches want that pipeline to continue. The best way to ensure that happens is for the Green Ridge coach to be a university track alum. There is a place on their team for you if you want it. I suggest you try the Steeplechase and the 10,000 meters for a couple of years. If it does not work out, you can become their team manager and learn about the sport from the inside."

"Wow. This is a real lot to think about. I feel like my life has just turned upside down."

"You have the whole summer to think about it and four years to decide about coaching. For what it is worth, you are a natural for it. You have a combination of great people skills and a knack for organization. You held this year's team together in tough times and steered it through troubled waters."

"I appreciate the words of support."

"Coach Mallory realized what you did this year and wanted to talk to you – but after the season was over to avoid distracting you from the task at hand. I promised him that I would talk to you if he did not make it to the end of the season. And here we are."

"Well, it certainly is an unexpected opportunity. I do want to discuss it with Mom and Dad, as well as Sue and Debbie – and Sean, Bruce, and Chuck. My track & field career may not be ending with a whimper after all."

Ted looked a bit puzzled but spoke:

"I can tell you that I have had a busy week as a law clerk. I want to run a few miles right now to clear my head. Care to join me?"

Artie thought for a moment, then smiled and spoke: "Yes, but let's make it longer - another long run!"

THE END

AFTERWARD

One question that readers often ask is what caused me to write track and field novels for young adults. The answer is that when I was in the seventh and eighth grade, I read sports novels for young adults that were in my school library. There were novels about baseball, football, and basketball, but none about track & field.

As I grew older, I noted that there were excellent track & field novels written and published for grown-ups, but still none written for young adults. This annoyed me. Finally, I started thinking about writing a track and field novel of my own for young adults.

Injuries had reduced my running to walking for exercise. During my walks, I formulated plot details in my mind. When I finally put my fingers to the keyboard, it was slow going to finish the first draft of *Relay* as my family, fulltime job, and track & field activities kept me plenty busy. I would try to write about a page a night. It would take most of a year to finish the first draft.

Even before *Relay* was in print, I had formulated the basic plot for the sequel and even then, it included Coach Mallory battling cancer. But then life got in the way some more before I could return to the keyboard. In 2013, the doctors diagnosed me with Multiple Myeloma which is cancer of the bone marrow. There is no permanent cure, but treatments can control it and put it in remission. With the help of my brilliant doctors and new treatments, I am still here over a decade later and have finally written the sequel. I have in mind one more novel set at Green Ridge High School. God willing, I will get that finished to complete a trilogy.

One more interesting thing happened between the time I wrote the first novel *Relay* and this sequel - smartphones and social media became commonplace. As a result, the world has changed significantly from when Ted Stewart attended high school in the first novel and when his younger brother Artie follows him about decade later in the sequel. Smartphones and social media play roles in the sequel.

Readers will also note that while the setting for high school track & field in the book is close to reality, I do have a few tweaks that I think would improve things. For example, the story takes place in a fictional state which rejects the 1,600 meters as an event in favor of a real Mile which is about 1,609 meters.

I also note that my first novel had two indoor district meets qualifying into the state indoor championships. After the book was published, the NJSIAA created four state sectional meets to do the same thing. I was ahead of my time!

Please note that I do not think that all football coaches are bad people. In fact, my cousin's husband has been both a football coach and track & field coach. Buddy McGurk is not based on any real individual. The characters and events of the story are fictious. Any resemblance to real people, living or dead, is coincidental.

Some readers may recognize my name from the positions I have held in USA Track & Field, its New Jersey Association, and the New Jersey Striders, Inc., which is a non-profit track & field club that I co-founded. The opinions expressed in either of the books are not necessarily those of any of these organizations and solely the responsibility of the author.

I would like to give words of thanks to many people.

I would like to thank my family. My parents and siblings have always been supportive of my track & field endeavors. My wife Cora inspires me daily and read the manuscript. My sons Eddie and Bill offered comments from a younger perspective.

I also give my thanks to members of the Striders "family" who offered comments and support, especially members of the Striders Board.

I also thank those that answered technical questions: Dan Pierce, Aaron Robinson, Mike Scott, Phil Moliere, and Tracy Sundlin.

And to my brother Joe, Roberta Anthes, Frank & Karen Collins, Randy Krakower and Frank & Judy Albert who read the manuscript and offered helpful comments. And my nephew Matt Koch was the model for the front cover illustration. Of course, any mistakes are my own.

    Finally, I thank Our Lord for seeing me through this project. I view every day as a blessing and hope my efforts on this book have been a constructive use of the time given me during my remission from Multiple Myeloma.